13

"Don't give up now, Red. You're almost home."

The voice rang deep and harsh against the walls of her stark prison, his tone distinctly American, not the more lilting intonations of her Thai captors.

Tori opened her eyes, met the gaze of her rescuer. Tall, fit and strong enough to kill without ever using the gun he wore strapped to his side. "What do you want?"

"You home and safe. So pay attention and do exactly what I say." He spoke as he pulled a slim tool from his pocket and used it to pop the lock on the manacles that bound Tori's wrists.

She did as she was told, the hope of escape overshadowing the questions that raced through her mind. Still, she hesitated as he helped her stand and led her to the door. "How do I know I can trust you?"

"What makes you think you have a choice?"

Books by Shirlee McCoy

Love Inspired Suspense

Die Before Nightfall #5
Even in the Darkness #14

Steeple Hill Trade

Still Waters #4

*Lakeview, Virginia

SHIRLEE McCOY

has always loved making up stories. As a child, she daydreamed elaborate tales in which she was the heroine—gutsy, strong and invincible. Though she soon grew out of her superhero fantasies, her love for storytelling never diminished. She knew early that she wanted to write inspirational fiction, and began writing her first novel when she was a teenager. Still, it wasn't until her third son was born that she truly began pursuing her dream of being published. Three years later she sold her first book. Now a busy mother of four, Shirlee is a homeschool mom by day and an inspirational author by night. She and her husband and children live in Maryland and share their house with a dog and a guinea pig. You can visit her Web site at www.shirleemccoy.com.

SHIRLEE McCOY

Even in the Darkness

Published by Steeple Hill Books™

STEEPLE HILL BOOKS

ISBN 0-373-87342-5

EVEN IN THE DARKNESS

This edition published by arrangement with Steeple Hill Books.

www.SteepleHill.com

Printed in U.S.A.

If I rise up on the wings of the dawn, if I settle on the far side of the sea, even there Your hand will guide me, Your right hand will hold me fast.

—*Psalms* 139:9–10

To my nieces and nephews who've already arrived—Joshua, Skylar, Danielle, Brianna, Trey, Jacob, Kaitlyn, John Paul, Elijah, Elijah, and Amirah—my life is brighter because you are in it. I love you all!

And to the one who hasn't arrived—baby Parker. Love begins on a breath of hope and rushes forward to embrace a dream. You are that dream. Safe travels, little one!

Special thanks to Kitty McCoy, proprietor of Kitty's Little Book Shoppe, and my biggest Smith Mountain Lake fan. Get the tea ready, I'm on my way!

Chapter One

The heat woke her. That and the silence. Until then there had been noise, movement, hushed voices—sounds both terrifying and comforting. Tori Riley levered up, biting back a groan as she forced herself to a sitting position. The room was the same—ugly and mean, its water-marked walls and rotted carpet reeking of age and neglect. Sunlight filtered through the dirt-crusted window, burying the room in stifling heat. Tori's throat was dry with it, and she reached for the cup that sat beside her on the floor, the shackles on her wrists clanging together.

The cup was empty. Just as it had been last night.

How much longer would they make her wait? She glanced toward the door, wishing it open, straining to hear above the pounding of her heart. The world beyond her prison seemed empty of life, the sounds she'd been hearing for the past few days absent.

Abandoned.

The word slipped into her mind; icy terror pumped through her veins. Did they know? Had they found the box? Or worse, had they found Melody?

The thought brought renewed energy. She threw her weight against the chains that held her, ignoring the harsh stab of pain in her wrists and the blood that seeped from the gashes there. Breath gasped from her lungs, her chest heaving as she struggled in an effort she knew was futile. Hadn't she tried before? Hadn't she failed? But she wouldn't fail now. She couldn't fail.

Sweat poured down her face, soaking the sweater she'd worn to keep warm on the plane ride home. Only she'd never made it to the airport, and now the heavy knit only intensified the heat and her panic.

Stop! Think! The words roared into her consciousness. How many times had her grandfather barked those words at her? Tori stilled her frantic movements and closed her eyes, letting herself picture Pops, the old farmhouse, the gray-blue lake shimmering in the distance. Home. She'd been a fool to run from it.

A sound drifted into the silence, a soft sigh of air that whispered of danger. Tori's eyes flew open. Someone was coming. Rescue? Or death? She counted seconds by the throb of the pulse in her throat, each beat a moment closer to whatever would come.

When the door opened and he stepped into the room, she knew.

Black pants, black shirt, black ski mask. Tall, fit and strong enough to kill without ever using the gun he wore strapped to his side.

Tori shrank back, then straightened, refusing the fear that coursed through her. "I told the others I mailed the box home."

He didn't speak, just stalked toward her, his movement fluid and pantherlike.

She tensed, wanting to run but knowing there was

nowhere to go. The only thing left to do was fight. She grabbed a length of chain in her hand, feeling the heft and weight of it, refusing to imagine the damage it could do.

He bent close, blue-green eyes striking against the black of his mask, his gaze softened by what looked like compassion.

Tori blinked, looked again, and the softness was gone, replaced by a hard determination that had her lifting the chain and swinging hard with her closed fist.

She should have known better. Dehydrated, weak from hunger, her body aching from what must have been days of torture, she was no match for the man's strength. His hand wrapped around hers, stopping its forward motion and forcing her fingers open. Dizzy from the effort, Tori slumped back against the wall, closing her eyes.

"Don't give up now, Red. You're almost home." The voice was deep and harsh, his tone distinctly American, not the more lilting intonations of her Thai captors.

Was he the ringleader? The boss? Did it matter?

She opened her eyes, met his gaze. "What do you want?"

"You home and safe. So pay attention and do exactly what I say." He spoke as he pulled a slim tool from his pocket and used it to pop the lock on the manacles that bound Tori's wrists.

She winced as metal pulled away from torn and bleeding flesh. Winced again as he lifted her wrists and looked at the raw wounds. "These'll scar, but you'll live."

He dropped her hands and pulled an envelope out from under his shirt. "Passport, plane tickets, money for a taxi. You leave this building, flag down the first taxi you see, and head for Chiang Mai International. Your flight leaves for Bangkok in half an hour. When you get there, don't leave the airport. You've got a flight home at eight this morning."

He thrust the envelope toward her and Tori grabbed it, hands trembling as she pulled out a passport with her picture and another woman's name, two plane tickets and a thousand baht. "Why are you helping me?"

"There's no time for questions. Just do what I tell you, and everything will be fine." He put a hand under her elbow and helped her to her feet. "Let your hair down so it covers the bruises on your face, and pull your sleeves over your wrists."

She did as she was told, the hope of escape overshadowing the questions that raced through her mind. Still, she hesitated as he led her to the door. "How do I know I can trust you?"

"What makes you think you have a choice?" With that he stepped out of the room.

Tori followed, hurrying along a dark corridor and into a trash-littered stairwell, down flight after flight of steps, then out into early-morning sunlight. The roar of Chiang Mai traffic filled her ears and the tangy scent of garlic and spices rode the air. A hundred yards away, Buddhist monks made their morning rounds, gathering the first portion of their supplicants' morning meals in the alms bowls they carried.

Tori took a step toward them, wanting desperately to make contact, and felt the heavy warmth of a hand on her shoulder. She turned, ready to fight for her freedom. It wasn't necessary.

Her rescuer dropped his hand, staring down into her face, his eyes blazing. "Remember what I said."

Then he stepped back inside the building and disappeared.

Tori dashed down the narrow street, heading in the direction the monks had disappeared. A flower vendor called out to her as she passed, holding up a bouquet of stunning purple and white orchids. She considered stopping, asking for help or directions, but rushed on instead. She didn't know her enemies, and couldn't be sure they weren't lurking somewhere close by. Up ahead the monks had paused to accept plastic bags filled with thick curry, the daily *bintabat* ritual providing them with food and Tori with the chance to overtake them.

Should she ask them for assistance?

No. Better to flag down a taxi and get as far from her captors as possible. She stood at the curb, raised her arm, wincing as pain shot through her ribs and side. Nothing was broken, though the bruises were enough to make deep breaths painful. Her captors had been careful, more interested in inflicting pain than in causing damage. That, at least, was a blessing.

A yellow cab pulled over and Tori clambered inside, ignoring the stench of sweat and tobacco that drifted from the torn vinyl seat. "How much to the nearest bus station?"

"One hundred baht." The driver spoke in heavily accented English, his craggy face solemn, his dark eyes meeting hers in the rearview mirror.

She nodded and settled back into the seat, trying to quiet the wild throb of her pulse as the taxi eased through traffic. In the distance a Buddhist temple speared the sky. Beautiful, exotic, different. When she'd come to Thailand three weeks ago that's what she'd been looking for—something more than the quiet, small-town life she led. Now she'd give anything to be home, riding in Pop's old Chrysler, traveling familiar roads, hearing the same stories she'd heard a hundred times before.

She could be. She had a passport, money, plane tickets. What she didn't have was the assurance that Melody was safe, and that was something she needed more than she needed home.

The taxi turned onto a narrow side street, and Tori glanced back. No cars followed. No motorcycles moved into place behind the cab. She wanted to believe she was safe, that the nightmare she'd been living was over. But that was a foolish hope. One she couldn't allow herself. She leaned forward. "How much longer?"

"Twenty minutes."

Twenty minutes too long. She needed to be in Mae Hong Son *now.* Anxiety clawed at her stomach, burning a fiery trail up her throat. She swallowed it down and tried to speak past her fear. "I've got a hundred baht more for you if you get me there in ten."

The driver nodded, turning down another street and picking up speed.

Hurry. Hurry. The words thundered through Tori's mind, a dizzying accompaniment to her racing pulse. How many days had passed since she'd given the box to the jeweler Chet Preteep? Five? Six? He'd told her then that it would take a week to make a locket like the one Tori wore, the one Melody had admired so much. A week, and then he'd put the locket in the rosewood trinket box Tori had provided and deliver it to Melody.

Tori glanced down at her wrist, looking for the date on her watch. But her watch had been taken, as had her locket and other jewelry. Was it already too late? Had the box been delivered? Tori shuddered at the thought of what that might mean for Melody. "What day is it?"

"Huh?"

"The day. Monday, Tuesday, Wednesday, Thursday."

"Yes."

"It's Thursday?"

"Yes."

Five days. Maybe she wasn't too late. She settled back into the seat, caught the driver eyeing her in the rearview mirror and lowered her head so that her hair fell forward. How bad were the bruises? She didn't dare try to get a look, could only imagine what the driver had seen. Would he talk to friends and family? Mention the bruised foreigner who had paid him double the fare to take her to the bus station? And if he did, how long would it be before the men who'd kidnapped her found her again?

Bone-deep cold, scared in a way she hadn't been in years, Tori tugged her sweater tight around aching ribs and tried desperately to come up with a plan. Her mind raced with images of Melody, beaten and tortured, her eyes filled with fear and pain. Tori had to get to Mae Hong Son before the box was delivered, had to make sure that the men who'd abducted her didn't get their hands on Melody.

She leaned her head back against the seat, trying to clear her mind, but it was too filled with terror and worry to focus. One minute she'd been packing, getting ready to return home. The next, she'd been chained to a wall, questions screamed into her face. Why?

She didn't have an answer. All she knew was that her longed-for trip to Thailand had turned into a nightmare, and because of that, Melody and her parents were in danger.

Please, God, keep them safe. Help me get there in time.

The prayer echoed through Tori's mind, a desperate plea. One she doubted would be answered. She'd lived life on her own terms for too long to expect help from God now. Tears clogged her throat and swam behind her eyes, but she refused to let them fall. Like praying, crying did no good. Clear thinking, determination—those were the things that would get her out of the mess she was in.

Up ahead, buses lined the road. A swarm of people hovered on the sidewalk waiting to board. Soon Tori would be waiting with them, ready to travel back to Mae Hong Son and the box that shouldn't have been a threat, but was.

"Bus terminal." The driver pulled up in front of the entrance.

Tori handed him payment and pushed open the door.

Despite the warmth of the day, she felt cold, fear shivering along her spine. She wouldn't let it stop her. With a deep, calming breath, she stepped out into the crowd.

"You have her?"

"Yeah." Noah Stone spoke into the cell phone as he followed his quarry inside the bus terminal.

"Guess your informant gave you good information."

"It pays to have contacts." Even if they were slimy as eels and twice as nasty.

"You at the airport?"

"'Fraid not."

"So she decided not to take the easy route home." Jack McKenzie's voice was calm, easy. As always.

"It's what we were banking on."

"You don't sound too happy about it."

"Using civilians doesn't sit well with me."

"Not a civilian. A courier, paid to pass information for the Wa."

"We don't know that for sure."

"And we don't know anything different. Her record might be clean, but there are plenty of others just like her who've gone bad."

"Can't argue with that." And he wouldn't try. Not when he'd known so many people who were clean on the surface and dirty deep down where it counted.

"One way or another, she's got the box. Once we've secured it, we'll give her a chance to tell her story."

"You're assuming we'll be able to secure it."

"With you here, it's a safe assumption."

"Guess that depends on whether Ms. Riley goes along with our plan." He watched as Tori stepped to a wall of pay phones and made a call.

"She will. The information on the box is worth millions. She won't leave the country without it."

"She's on the move. I'll keep in touch." He slipped the phone into his pocket and stepped into line at a ticket counter, his gaze tracking Tori as she stepped into a line half the building away. She stood with her head high, her shoulders straight. Only someone looking closely would notice the bluish welts on her face, or the way her hand shook as she paid for a ticket and shoved it into her pocket.

She might be in deep with Lao, perhaps deep enough to double-cross him and grab the box, but Noah doubted it. There'd been something in her eyes when he'd freed her—a softness that seemed too genuine to fake. That, and a quiet desperation that surpassed greed or fear for herself. She was terrified, but heading back into the fray. Why?

Her daughter. It was the obvious answer, one Noah couldn't discount. If Tori was what she appeared to be—a small-town veterinarian who'd come to Thailand to visit the daughter she'd given up in an open adoption thirteen years before—then her first instinct would be to ensure the safety of the girl.

If she was what she seemed.

The DEA had good reason to suspect otherwise. Noah would reserve judgment. He'd follow Tori, find out what had sent her running from safety. Then he'd know more about her motivation and her guilt.

A white bus rattled to a stop in front of the terminal and Tori hurried outside. Noah followed, holding back as she purchased a straw hat from a vendor. Then he followed her onto the bus. One quick glance found Tori squeezed into a back seat between two Thai women. From her position she'd have a good view out the back window. Maybe she thought she'd catch a glimpse of any pursuers. If so, she had no idea the caliber of men who'd soon be scouring the countryside. Noah did. The ache in his left shoulder and back were a grim reminder of just how deadly men like Lao could be.

The bus lurched forward as Noah slid into a front seat. Several people still stood in the aisle, clinging to handholds and swaying with the motion. In other circumstances Noah would offer a seat to an elderly passenger as a sign of respect and honor. Not today. His black hair and tan skin might blend with the Thai passengers, but his height and large build gave him away as a foreigner. At this point, he couldn't afford to call attention to himself.

He settled back into the seat, listening to chatter and laughter, catching phrases and words—English and Thai, as well as several other languages he wasn't as familiar with. It didn't take long to determine the bus's destination. Mae Hong Son. A seven-hour drive. Longer if the bus made tourist stops. The knowledge should have eased some of Noah's tension, but adrenaline pulsed through him, warning him that time was running out.

He glanced back, eyeing the cars and trucks that followed behind the bus. He'd been hoping for a few hours' lead time. Had thought the men he'd left bound and gagged in the building where he'd found Tori would need longer than that to free themselves.

He'd been wrong.

He didn't question the knowledge. It was part of who he was. Part of what made him a survivor in an industry where death lurked around every corner. The other part was faith—a deep understanding that all that happened was choreographed by God—who was much more powerful than any government, agency or enemy.

It was that, more than anything, that had drawn Noah out of an early retirement and back into a game he no longer wanted to play; it was a deep knowing that he had to take the assignment. That something vital depended on it. Something beyond securing the box and stopping the distribution of millions of dollars' worth of heroin.

Maybe once Tori led him to their destination he'd get some answers. Noah wasn't counting on it.

Chapter Two

"We share?" The young Thai woman who sat beside Tori held out a bottle of Coke, her face wreathed in a smile.

"No. Thank you." Tori's own smile felt more like a grimace, her voice gritty from fatigue and dehydration. Despite her parched throat and empty stomach, she hadn't dared get off the bus at the last tourist stop. Not when a dark sedan and white pickup truck had been following the bus since its first stop earlier in the day.

"You come visit me in Mae Hong Son, yes?"

"If I can. I'll only be there for a short time."

"You come. We will be there soon. Ten minutes. Your family will meet you, yes?"

"No. I'm meeting a friend." Tori shifted in her seat, turning away from the other woman, hoping, as she had been hoping for the past seven hours, to discourage conversation. So far she hadn't been successful. Which meant eventually other people would know she'd been on this bus.

Sweat trickled down her temple, and she used the

sleeve of her sweater to brush it away, ignoring the palsied trembling of her hand. Just a few more minutes and she'd be in Mae Hong Son. Then what? She glanced out the back window of the bus, saw the sedan a few cars back. The pickup was nowhere in sight, though Tori had a feeling it still followed. How much time did she have? Could she make it off the bus, make it to Chet's jewelry shop before they caught her?

She bit her lip, forcing back the panic that threatened to overtake her. She'd do what she had to do to escape the men who followed her. There was no other choice. Then she'd make her way to Chet's shop. If he had the box, she'd take it and run. If not, she'd try to call the clinic again and hope that this time someone answered.

The bus slowed and came to a stop, the cessation of movement bringing Tori upright in her seat. She craned her neck, trying to see what lay ahead. A green government truck sat on the side of the road, two armed military officers waving motorists over.

"What's going on?"

"No worries." The woman next to her patted Tori's arm and seemed unperturbed, but Tori's heart beat in double time, her hands clenched into fists.

One of the soldiers stepped aboard the bus and leafed through the driver's paperwork. Then scanned the passengers, his dark gaze resting on one person after another. Tori closed her eyes and feigned sleep, hoping to hide her eyes and the terror she knew shone there. For the second time in hours, she tried to pray, the knee-jerk reaction to terror reminding her of the desperate pleas she'd offered up as a child. Pleas that had gone unanswered.

This time it seemed God was on her side. A few seconds after the soldier entered the bus, he stepped back outside, waving the driver on and moving toward the next car in line. The sedan was three cars back, the pickup truck right behind it. Now was Tori's chance to lose anyone following.

She didn't hesitate, just waited until the bus rounded a curve in the road, and stood, hurrying up to the driver. "Stop, please. I need to get off here."

He shook his head. "Sorry. No stops."

"I have friends in the area. They said I'd be able to get off the bus before I reached town." *Please, please, let him stop the bus and let me off.*

For a moment she thought he'd refuse. Then he shrugged, downshifted and eased the bus to the side of the road.

"Thank you." She didn't wait for his reply, just stepped outside.

Warm sun. Damp earth. The harsh call of some creature in the jungle. The sound, the scent, the feel of freedom. Tori waited as the bus pulled away, watching to be sure it didn't stop again, that no one else got off. Then she slipped into the thick foliage that lined the road, pulled off her hat, eased down into tall grass and waited.

The sedan passed first, speeding by in a flurry of sound and motion. The pickup was next, coming more slowly. Tori could see it through the grass, inching along the highway. She sank down, touching her cheek to the cool, damp ground.

Terror brought the world into sharp focus. A centipede scurried near Tori's hand. Flies buzzed near her wrists, landing on the broken flesh. She didn't dare brush them away. The musty aroma of rich earth filled her nose. Grass and leaves whispered an almost silent tune. And the rumbling chug of the pickup's engine finally faded away. Time to move. Mae Hong Son was a few miles north. Soon there would be houses, people, someone willing to give her a ride to Chet's jewelry shop.

She forced herself up. Her body ached from fatigue and from bruises on top of bruises. Moving hurt. Walking any distance would be torture. She'd do it anyway. For Melody. For Melody's parents. For herself. She couldn't bear it if something happened to the Raymonds because of her.

Already, the sun rode low in the sky, lengthening the shadows and darkening the landscape. By nightfall most of the shops in Mae Hong Son would be closed. If she didn't hurry, she'd be too late to speak with Chet.

She started jogging, jagged pain slicing through her side with each step. She wanted to sit for a minute, catch her breath, but there wasn't time, so she kept going, passing stilt-legged huts with chickens scratching at the dirt beneath, wide green rice paddies that shone brilliant green in the fading light. A water buffalo meandered through hip-tall grass, its wide nostrils flaring, a brown-skinned child perched on its back.

Up ahead was a busy tourist stop. Tori had been there before, had bought sweet rhambutan from a vendor. For the right price she might convince one of them to take her into Mae Hong Son.

She approached from the back of the property, the sounds of voices, engines and the strident call of an elephant drifting on the air around her. When she reached the corner of the building, she paused. Once she stepped into the open, she'd be vulnerable again. Unfortunately, time was too limited for her to stand and think through her options. She'd have to round the corner and take her chances in the crowd.

She took a deep breath, tensed to move and was pulled backward with one sharp tug on her sweater. She went fighting, fists swinging, mind blank of all but one thought—escape. An arm snaked around her waist and a hand slammed over her mouth, cutting off a scream.

"Stop struggling." The words were hissed into her ear, the grip never loosening.

She responded by struggling harder, imagining a needle poised over her flesh, a stab, and then oblivion. That's how they'd taken her before. It wouldn't happen again. Not if she could help it.

She twisted, trying to throw her attacker off balance. Pain speared across her rib cage, stealing her breath. Pinpricks of light flashed in front of her eyes, she swayed, and was suddenly being supported instead of restrained.

"Whoa. No passing out, Red."

Red? Tori stiffened.

"That's better. Now hold still and be quiet. There's company out there. Not the kind either of us wants to meet." Noah didn't loosen his grip as he spoke, nor did he remove the hand he held over Tori's mouth. Her tense muscles warned that she was waiting for an opportunity to break free, and that was something he couldn't allow. Not yet. Later, when he had her safely away from the men who were hunting her, he'd let her go again. See where she'd been heading before she'd almost walked into Lao's trap. For now he'd stay close.

She twisted in his arms, trying once again to break free as he edged them away from the building. He ignored her struggles, ignored the heel that barely missed his knee, but he couldn't ignore her terror. Her body shook with it, her heart pounding so hard he could feel it in the pulse point near her jaw.

That, more than anything, had him tightening his grip and leaning close to her ear. "You want me to let you go?"

She didn't nod, didn't acknowledge the question in any way.

He hadn't expected her to. "I will, but know this—you scream, and there's a good possibility we won't live to see tomorrow. You run, and I'll have you before you take five steps, then I'll tie you up and gag you until we're somewhere safe." An idle threat, but she didn't need to know that.

With that he slid his arm from around her waist and eased his hand from her mouth, remaining close, not allowing her enough distance for a head start if she decided to run.

For a moment she didn't move. When she did, it was a quick spin in his direction, her hair flying in a cloud of burnished red. "Who are you? What do you want from me?"

"Noah Stone. And what I want is you on the plane that left for the States a few hours ago. Since I can't have that, I'll settle for putting some distance between us and the people searching for you." That much was true. The rest would have to wait.

"That's no answer."

"It's as much of one as I can give. Come on. Let's get out of here."

"And go where?" Her voice sounded raspy and dry, her eyes dark fire against pallid skin.

"A place where we don't have to worry about the bad guys finding us." He reached down, picked up the hat that had fallen from Tori's head during their struggle and handed it to her.

"For all I know, *you're* one of the bad guys."

"If I were, we wouldn't be standing here talking."

"I can't know that." She stared him down, the bruises on her cheek and jaw an ugly reminder of all she'd been through.

"And I don't have time to prove it. The bus you were on made it to Mae Hong Son. The men who were following know you weren't on it. Now they're backtracking. It won't take long for one of them to find us." He grabbed her hand, tugging her farther away from the tourist stop.

She didn't resist, though he had no doubt she wanted to. She'd probably weighed the odds of escape and decided not to waste the energy trying. Good. Her cooperation would make their journey less difficult.

Despite her obvious fatigue, she matched Noah's stride, not giving in to the pain he'd seen in her eyes. Jaw set, hair a wild halo of curls around her face, the straw hat clutched in her hand, she looked both strong and vulnerable. An interesting combination and nothing like the hardened, experienced drug courier Noah had expected when he'd been asked to take this assignment.

She must have sensed his gaze. She turned to meet it, the fear and anger he'd seen minutes ago masked by a calm facade. "I know you want the box. I don't have it. I sent it to the States."

"Yeah?"

"Yeah. So maybe you should head that way yourself."

"And leave you to wander around Mae Hong Son alone? I don't think so."

She laughed at that, the sound harsh. "Your concern is touching, but I can manage just fine on my own."

He let his gaze linger on her bruises, then drop to the sleeves of her sweater where blood had tinged the white knit pink. "Doesn't look like it to me."

Tori couldn't argue with that. She knew how she must look—tired, bruised, defeated. But her appearance wouldn't hinder her intentions. And what she intended was escape. She slanted a glance in Noah's direction, wondering if escape would even be possible. Black hair gleaming in the sun, a dark beard shadowing his jaw, he seemed strong and confident, a man used to making decisions and taking charge. She'd known plenty of men like him—men willing to say or do anything to get what they wanted. Luckily, Tori had learned her lesson hard and well. No way would she trust Noah. Not when so much was at stake.

An image of Melody flashed through her mind—fresh-faced, laughing, filled with the kind of spontaneous joy Tori had never been allowed. The thought of how easily that could change sent her pulse racing. She had to get to her daughter. Had to grab the box and run as far and as fast as she could.

"Don't even think about it." His voice held quiet authority, his expression not changing as he tugged her closer to his side.

"I wasn't thinking about anything."

"You were thinking about running. Save us both the time and energy—don't bother."

There was nothing to say to that, so she didn't speak at all. Not that she had the energy to do more than keep up with Noah. He moved with a long, brisk stride, not slowing his pace as they stepped onto a narrow, paved road that led to the outskirts of Mae Hong Son. Rundown houses and faded buildings stood like weary sentinels to either side, their long shadows touching the road with darkness. In the distance, deep green mountains brushed the sky, shrouded in mist and mystery. A few people hurried along a cracked and broken sidewalk, too rushed to notice the strangers in their midst. Or maybe they noticed and chose not to show it. An odd thought, but one Tori couldn't shake.

Nor could she shake the feeling that she and Noah were being watched, that every step they took was being monitored. She glanced around, tense with nerves, and was surprised by the warmth of Noah's breath as he spoke close to her ear. "Relax. They're friends. Of a sort."

"Who?"

"The people watching us."

So he felt it, too. Tori wasn't sure if she should be relieved or even more worried. "Who are they?"

"No one we need to worry about. An acquaintance of mine owns some property around here. He likes to know who's coming and going."

"And that's supposed to make me feel better?"

"It should. There's no love lost between Hawke and Lao."

"I don't suppose you're going to tell me who Hawke and Lao are?"

"Hawke is a man I've worked with a few times. Lao is a suspected member of the Wa, a militia group based across the border in Myanmar. Lao's the one you took the box from."

"I didn't take the box. I bought it."

"You have the box. He wants it back."

"Why? It's a box. Pretty. Expensive. But just a box." She expected him to ignore her question. Instead he stopped short, pulling her around to face him.

His face was granite hard in the fading light, his eyes the blue-green of angry ocean waves. "I'd like to think you believe that."

"I do."

He watched her, his expression unreadable, then turned and started walking again.

"I'm telling the truth. I saw a rosewood trinket box at a tourist shop when I was visiting Wat Doi Kong Mu. It was broken, so the clerk brought one out from the back." The words spilled out, and Tori bit her lip to keep from saying more.

"And was killed for his efforts."

"What?"

"Story on the street is he was robbed and beaten to death. Truth is, Lao doesn't take kindly to having his plans ruined. Especially not when the Wa is involved. You might want to keep that in mind."

The words might be either threat or warning. Neither was necessary. Tori knew the danger she was in, the danger Melody would be in if she had the box and the people who'd abducted Tori found out about it.

Lao. The name was unfamiliar, the taste of it bitter against Tori's tongue. She raked a hand through her hair, wincing as her fingers caught in tangled curls. Nothing made sense. The well-ordered life she'd been living was suddenly a bizarre dance whose steps she didn't know. She'd have to learn them fast if she was going to survive. And the only way to learn was to ask questions, get answers and weed out the truth from the lies. “Where did you say we were going?”

“A safe place.”

“Safe from Lao.”

“That’s right.”

“And will I be safe from you?”

“Safe enough.”

“Are you always so talkative?”

He shot her a sideways look meant to still her words. “Are you?”

“No.”

“Now would be a good time to go back to your old habits.”

He picked up the pace, leading the way through a dim alley, then across several narrow streets. Jaw set, he turned into a dark, dank walkway between two buildings. “Stay close through here. You get lost and you might never find your way out.”

“Right.” The word rasped out, the deepening shadows and dingy grayness of the surrounding walls enough to convince Tori that she should do as told.

The air reeked of sewage and rot. Bags of garbage overflowed with spoiled food and decaying trash. The ground teemed with living things, insects and lizards darting away as Tori and Noah moved forward. Geckos clung to the cinderblock sides of the buildings, their tan bodies scurrying into motion.

Not a place to linger. Especially not when insects and lizards didn’t seem to be the only creatures thriving in the garbage-clogged alley. Tori could feel the weight of human gazes following the progress she and Noah were making. She wondered who they were, where they were hiding, when they would show themselves. *If* they would show themselves. She imagined the whiz of a bullet, the pain she'd feel as it slammed into her flesh.

"This is it."

Noah's words pulled Tori from her macabre thoughts, and she turned her attention to the low stone wall and wrought-iron gate in front of them. Both looked new and well tended. The property that Noah's friend owned? Probably. Tori didn't know who the friend was, but the fact that he and Noah were pals had already biased her against him.

Noah put a hand on the gate and pushed it open. "Let's go."

He stepped through. Tori straightened her spine, clenched her jaw to stop its trembling and followed.

Chapter Three

Thick mist shrouded the courtyard, making monsters out of shadows and trees, and painting the world in eerie light. Noah led Tori to the front of a two-story stucco building and pounded his fist against a faded wood door. Then they waited. Tori stood close beside him, her tension obvious in the soft, quick gasp of her breath. When the door swung open, she started, her hand grasping his arm, then dropping away as if she'd suddenly realized what she was doing.

"Come on." He pulled her inside a dark room, felt more than saw someone move to close the door. Then the hard barrel of a gun pressed tight under his jaw. He didn't flinch, didn't try to pull his weapon. Just waited.

"*Sawatdee khrap,* my friend." The words were spoken in rapid-fire Thai.

Noah answered in the same. "If we're friends, why the gun?"

"Precaution. Why are you here?"

"Hawke owes me a favor. I've come to collect."

"We'd heard you retired."

"Depends on who you ask."

The gun dropped away and a light flicked on.

A Thai man leaned against one wall, his expression more curious than suspicious. Not Hawke. Apirak Koysayodin—one of the few men Hawke trusted.

"Who's the woman?"

"She's a friend."

"Hawke won't like that you've brought her here." There was no heat in the words or in the dark gaze he swept over Tori.

Her fingers tapped a fast rhythm against her thigh. Her gaze darted from Apirak to the door. Probably wondering how easy it would be to bolt across the room and escape.

Noah grabbed her hand, holding her in place as he turned his attention back to Apirak. "Sometimes we have choices, sometimes we don't. My friend and I need some information."

"You want to know about the snakes that are slithering through Mae Hong Son."

"That's right."

"There aren't many. Ten. Twelve."

"What are they hunting?"

"A woman. An American with red hair and brown eyes. It seems she took something from Sang Lao. Something he's desperate to retrieve."

That confirmed what the DEA's informant had reported. A local businessman, Lao had been suspected of drug trafficking for years. So far he'd eluded the DEA and the Royal Thai Police. It looked like his luck might be running out. "What about the Wa?"

"We've yet to see any of them."

"That's something to be thankful for."

"A small thing. And something much bigger to worry about."

"What?"

"There's a price on your friend's head. Fifty thousand baht." Again he glanced at Tori, his eyes speculative.

"A lot of money."

"Yes, but most people here despise Sang Lao and wouldn't help him for all the riches in the world."

"It's the rest of the people I'm worried about. We'll need an escort out of town."

"It's been arranged."

"Hawke's ahead of the game."

"Your people are not the only ones who want to bring Lao down. Hawke has been patient. It seems his time might be at hand." Apirak spoke as he stepped to the door and pulled it open. "There's a car waiting for you at the entrance to Market Street. It will take you wherever you want to go."

"Tell Hawke we're even."

"It will take more than this for Hawke to think he's repaid the debt he owes you." With that, the light went out and Apirak disappeared.

"What's going on? What did he say?" Tori's words were just above a whisper.

"Not here." Noah tugged on her hand, pulling her outside.

"Well?"

"There's a price on your head. Fifty thousand baht."

If the news surprised her, she didn't show it, just nodded, her dark eyes shadowed. "Now what?"

"We go meet our ride."

"Ride?"

"We're going back to Chiang Mai. It's time for you to go home."

If he wanted a reaction, he got one. Her body tensed, and he thought she might run. Instead, she nodded. "Good idea."

The words were hollow, empty of enthusiasm.

"For someone who's running for her life, you don't seem very happy about getting an escort home."

"It's the escort I'm opposed to. Not the trip home."

"Sorry. You're stuck with me." Until you decide to make your move. He didn't say the last part, though he was thinking it. If Tori was guilty, she'd make a break for the box eventually. When she did, Noah would be right behind her.

They moved back into the dank walkway, the silence heavy between them. Tori fought the urge to break it, afraid if she started talking she'd say too much, reveal more than she should. With her wrists throbbing, her head pounding and what few ideas she had muddled by fatigue, Tori figured the best she could offer herself and Melody was silence.

Noah glanced her way, his face cold and unyielding. "It would save us both a lot of trouble if you'd tell me where the box is."

"I already told you—"

"I've heard that story before. Why don't we try a new one?"

"Why don't you try telling me who you are and why you freed me? Why you want the box and what you're going to get out of having it? Maybe then we'll have more to talk about."

Noah smiled, a feral curve of his lips that sent a shiver down Tori's spine. "Seems we're at a stalemate."

She shrugged, determined not to waste more time talking. Her energy was waning and she still had a long way to go.

"Nothing to say, Red?"

"Tori."

"What's that?"

"My name is Tori. Not Red." She bit out the words, angry with herself for responding to his bait, angry with Noah for refusing to tell her who he worked for and why he wanted the box.

"Tori. Red. It won't matter if Lao gets his hands on you again." The coldness in his voice chilled Tori to the core, but she couldn't let it shake her resolve.

She might not know who Noah was, but she knew what he wanted. Unfortunately for him, she didn't plan to give it to him. Not when doing so might lead danger to Melody and her parents. Better to retrieve the box and bring it to the U.S. embassy in Bangkok. Let anyone who wanted it follow her there. Including Noah. Including the man called Lao. If they weren't one and the same. She glanced at Noah. Was it possible he *was* the ringleader of the men who'd kidnapped her? That he'd freed her because he'd known she would go after the box? And once he had the box, would he kill her or let her live?

Tori had no intention of staying with him long enough to find out.

Up ahead the alley opened into a wide street, the sound of motorcycle engines growing louder with each step. Tori's muscles tensed as she and Noah walked out into an open-air market colored amber by the fading sun. People milled about, buying hot noodle soup and succulent fruit from vendors. A normal, busy evening.

But somewhere in the midst of it danger lurked. Tori felt it in the churning of her stomach and the goose bumps that leaped to attention on her arms. Her captors were out there, waiting.

She glanced around, trying to put a face to the warning that hummed along her nerves. That's when she saw the hotel. Two stories, well maintained. She knew it immediately. She'd been shopping on this street before. Market Place. Market Road. She couldn't remember the name, but it didn't matter. What mattered was that Chet's store was just a few blocks away, an easy walk. All she had to do was lose her escort.

Noah scanned the crowd, his face set in hard lines as he searched for signs of trouble. She could run now, make a break for it while he was distracted. Before she could take a step away, he grabbed a fistful of her sweater. One hard tug brought her up against his side. Then he dropped his arm across her shoulders, and any hope of escape was gone.

"There's the car. Let's go." He urged her toward a dark sedan that idled in front of the market. A man leaned against its fender, a dragon tattoo circling his biceps, a machete sheathed at his waist. He straightened as they approached, offering a brief nod in Noah's direction. "Hawke says you need a ride."

"Hawke's right."

"Where to?"

"The airport."

"Get in." He pulled the back door open and everything inside Tori stilled. This was it. Her chance. Maybe the only one she'd get. All she had to do was slide across the seat, shove the door open and jump out the other side of the car. With the crowd bustling around, she might just get lost in the hubbub and escape.

"Go on." Noah spoke close to her ear, his breath warm against her neck, his arm lifting from her shoulders. There was something in his tone—a question or a dare.

There wasn't time to wonder what it meant. She scooted across the seat, her muscles stiff, her fingers itching to try the door handle. She waited as Noah said a few more words to their driver. Then, as Noah put his hand on the door frame, bent down his head and started to get into the car, Tori shoved the door open and jumped out. Two steps took her into the street, her feet pounding against the pavement as she dodged motorcycles and tuk-tuks, not daring to look back.

Noah watched her go, grim satisfaction not quite overriding worry. Courier or not, Tori was an American woman in a place she didn't know well, running from men who'd do more than torture her if they got their hands on her again. And she was an easy mark. She'd forgotten her hat, and her hair shone deep burgundy in the fading light, her tall, slim figure towering over most of the Thais.

Noah fought the urge to race after her and drag her back to the safety of the car. The plan Jack had outlined was simple, almost foolproof. Free the courier from Lao's prison, follow her to the box, secure the information and bring both the woman and the box back to DEA headquarters in Chiang Mai. Easy. Except Noah wasn't convinced Tori was the courier.

"You going after her?" Simon Morran looked relaxed as Noah stepped back out of the car, but there was a tension in him that said he was ready for action.

"Just giving her a head start."

"Don't make it too much of one. Sang Lao's men are eager to get their hands on her."

"I don't plan to let her out of my sight. Tell your brother I appreciate the ride." He didn't bother with goodbye, just started across the street, ignoring the beep of a horn and the unhappy glare of a tuk-tuk driver.

"Better watch it. You get run over and who's going to protect the woman?"

Simon had moved into step beside him. Except for the coldness in his face, he looked nothing like Hawke. Rumor had it they were stepbrothers. Could be it was true. Not that it mattered. What mattered was that Simon was as quick and lethal as his brother. A strong ally and a dangerous adversary. And for that day, he and Noah were on the same side.

Noah looked at the other man, made a quick decision. "You up for a game of cat and mouse?"

"Got nothing better to do. Besides, Hawke said I'm supposed to get you out of the city."

"I could use another set of eyes and ears."

"We trying to catch her?"

"Trying to keep her safe without letting her know we're following."

"That shouldn't be hard. She isn't even looking back."

It was true. Tori raced through the crowd with blind determination, perhaps hoping that speed would be enough to keep her safe. After a few blocks, she paused, glanced around and then pushed open the door of a store.

"She's going into that shop. You know the owners?"

"An elderly widow and her son. Quiet, honest people."

"Not friends of Sang Lao then. Let's split up. You take the back, I'll take the front."

Simon nodded, breaking away from Noah and disappearing around the side of the building.

The shop looked ordinary—a jewelry smith with sparkling wares displayed in wide, clean windows. Was the box here? Perhaps being kept by a partner of Tori's who had yet to be discovered by the DEA or Lao? It didn't seem likely. Not if what Simon said about the owners was true. Not if Noah's gut instinct about Tori was right. Still, his body hummed with anticipation as he moved past the store and took a seat at a bus stop a few buildings away. From there he had a clear view of the shop door. If Tori walked outside, he'd know. And if any unwanted company arrived, he'd stop them before they made it into the store. Noah prayed it wouldn't come to that. Not here, on a busy street with so many people around. If it did, though, he'd be ready.

Tori stood in the tiny bathroom she'd been led to and splashed her face with water. A small, hazy mirror sat above the sink, the face reflected in it one she barely recognized. Bruised, hollow-eyed, she looked nothing like the healthy veterinarian she knew herself to be. She patted a soft towel against her cheek, wincing a little as the fabric brushed against her swollen jaw. Every bone in her body ached, but nothing compared to the ache in her heart. Chet had rushed to complete the locket, hoping to please both Tori and Melody's family, and had delivered it to the clinic yesterday. Now there was no chance that the teen wouldn't be touched by the evil that had touched Tori.

If anything happened to Melody…

But it wouldn't. Tori wouldn't let it.

A soft knock sounded at the door, and she pulled it open.

"My son will come soon." Parinyah Preteep spoke quietly, her face lined with age and worry.

"Thank you. I'm sorry for bringing this trouble to you."

"The trouble is no fault of yours. Here—" she handed Tori a thick fold of fabric "—you put on."

Tori shook out the garment—a dark blue gown that looked similar to a nun's habit—took off her sweater and pulled the material on over her T-shirt and jeans.

"Now this." Parinyah held out a silky white scarf. "Over hair."

Tori draped the scarf over her hair and let the older woman fashion it into a head covering that wrapped around the lower part of her face. When she glanced in the mirror, she could see that nothing but her eyes were visible.

"Now you ready."

"Thank you."

"Go safely and have peace." The words were a benediction, and Tori squeezed the other woman's hand, wishing she had something more than thanks to offer.

Somewhere outside a horn beeped, and Parinyah hurried to the back door of the shop, calling out a question as she pulled it open. She got an answer, then turned to Tori and waved her forward. "Chet says okay. He sees no one outside."

Tori wasn't sure that meant much. Noah had watched her, followed her, been close enough to grab her, and she hadn't known he was there until it was too late. But she couldn't think on that. She needed to focus her energy on getting to Melody, making sure she and her family were safe. Then getting the box away from them and to the consulate. She'd worry about the rest after that.

A gray-green mist touched the air with moisture, and Tori shivered as she stepped out the door of the shop. Clothes hung from lines that stretched from building to building across the alley, colorful banners limp in the moist air. Voices called back and forth, children giggling and laughing as they chased each other barefoot through the alley. Tori kept her head bowed as she moved toward Chet Preteep, whose short, wiry frame balanced on a motorbike that didn't look big enough to carry its driver, let alone a passenger.

Tori fought back hysterical laughter. "Will I fit on there?"

"Yes. Like this." Parinyah sat sideways behind her son, looping an arm around his waist before sliding off again, her movements surprisingly spry for a woman that Tori knew was almost eighty years old.

"All right. I can do that." Tori did as she'd been shown, her arm around Chet's waist, holding on with a grip just tight enough to keep her from falling. "Thank you again."

"You take care of Melody."

"I will."

"Ready?" Chet glanced back, his dark eyes filled with worry.

"Yes."

He spoke a few quiet words to his mother, then started the motor and headed down the narrow road that ran behind the shop. Several people shouted greetings as the motorbike passed. Some seemed curious, perhaps wondering about Tori. Luckily they wouldn't remember much about her appearance. Tori was thankful for that. Thankful that Parinyah had thought of the scarf and the long garment that hid Tori's clothes.

Chet stopped the motorbike at the entrance to a wide, paved road that buzzed with motorcycles, tuk-tuks and a few cars. All were driving at speeds much greater than what Tori imagined the motorbike could achieve. Her grip tightened on Chet. "Is it safe?"

He either didn't understand, or chose not to answer. The motorbike edged closer to the road, the engine humming impatiently.

Tori shifted, trying to balance her weight more evenly, and felt the hair on the back of her neck stand on end.

Someone was watching.

Slowly, easily, as if she were glancing back for no reason at all, she turned to look. The heavy mist and fading light concealed more than they revealed, and at first Tori saw nothing. Then a dark figure near the corner of a building caught her eye—tall, broad, deceptively relaxed. She didn't need to see clearly to know who it was. Noah. She knew it as surely as she knew he had let her escape. That he had planned all along to let her go so that he could follow her to the box.

Her suspicions about him had been correct.

It shouldn't have surprised her. She'd been betrayed too many times to expect anything different. First by Melody's father, his flowery words and promises of love empty of meaning. Then by Joe. Kind, sweet Joe. The perfect partner, his strong faith more than making up for Tori's floundering one. He'd seemed flawless until she'd caught him kissing a choir member. And then there'd been Kyle. She didn't dare think of him. On the hollow emptiness that came from being betrayed one too many times.

No, Tori wasn't surprised by Noah's lies and betrayal. How could she be? Betrayal was all she'd ever known.

The motorbike lurched forward, a car horn blasted a warning, and Tori was too busy hanging on for dear life to think about Noah or her own disappointment.

Chapter Four

The road to the Raymonds' clinic wound uphill through dense jungle. There were no streetlights to guide the way, and already the thin ribbon of pavement seemed to disappear in the deepening shadows. Without the headlight from the motorbike it would be impossible to see what lay ahead. That was fine. Tori was more concerned about what lay behind.

She turned her head, peering into evening gloom. She saw nothing. More importantly, she heard nothing.

"No one follows?" Chet spoke above the chug of the bike's engine, the worry in his voice obvious.

"No. We're fine." For how long? Tori might have had a head start, but Noah wouldn't be far behind. Even if she'd eluded him completely, it wouldn't take long for him to find out where she was headed. Mae Hong Son wasn't much more than a small town, and Tori had visited it several times with the Raymonds. Those visits would have been noticed, talked about.

As if he sensed her worries, Chet patted the arm she still had wrapped around his waist. "No worries. The

Raymonds will be fine. They have many friends in Mae Hong Son. Many people they have helped."

"Maybe so, but money can be a powerful incentive." She thought of the bamboo huts that lined the outskirts of the town, the agricultural economy so reliant on weather. Who wouldn't be tempted by a secure future and a life of ease?

"Money is less important here than honor. Our people will protect the Raymonds because it is the right thing to do."

Tori wished she had as much faith in human nature. She didn't. "How much farther to the clinic?"

"Maybe ten minutes."

"Is there any way to get there more quickly?"

"No. This is the only road in. There are a few trails through the jungle, but taking them at dusk would be foolish and dangerous."

"My entire trip to Thailand seems foolish and dangerous right now. If I'd stayed home, none of this would have happened."

"It's never good to look back and think of what we might have done differently. You came to Thailand on good faith that you would be safe. Unfortunately, Thailand, like any other country, has its share of criminals. I'm sorry you had the misfortune to run into them."

"I survived. That's what matters." That, and making sure Melody stayed safe.

"My mother said you were taken from your hotel room?"

"Yes. In Chiang Mai."

"And the people who took you wanted the box?"

"That's what they were asking for."

"Strange. It is a nice piece, but not valuable. The locket you had made is worth much more."

"I know. It doesn't make sense."

"A worry for another time, I think. For now, we think only of getting to the clinic. Then we'll get the box and get it far from the Raymonds."

"When we get to the clinic, I want you to turn around and go home. I can't put you in any more danger than I already have."

"The Raymonds have been my friends for five years. They've taught me English, taught me about God, shown me and my family true kindness and Christian love. I won't turn my back on them during this trouble. Nor will I turn my back on someone they care about."

There was no sense in arguing. Despite Chet's passionate words and clear regard for the Raymonds, Tori couldn't let him get any more involved in her troubles than he already was. If he insisted, she would have no choice but to sneak away from the clinic without his notice. It wouldn't be difficult. If she could escape a man like Noah Stone, she could escape the loyal, trusting man who now helped her. *But you didn't escape Noah. He's behind you. Following. Waiting for a chance to grab the box. And when he gets it...then what?*

The thoughts worried at Tori's mind as the motorbike sped on. How much time did she have before Noah caught up with her? Probably not as much as she needed. She glanced back, but the road was still empty. To either side, towering trees and thick foliage bristled with life; nocturnal animals emerging from their daytime sleep, diurnal animals tucking themselves away for the night. If Tori were at home, she'd be starting her day, heading to the veterinary clinic to see her first patient. Instead she was running for her life.

She blinked back hot tears and shoved aside thoughts of home. Right now, her focus had to be on getting the box and carrying it far away from Melody. There'd be time for everything else later.

"There. The clinic." Chet gestured to the right where bright yellow lights spilled through the trees, the sight a welcome relief.

Seconds later, he rounded a steep curve and pulled the motorbike up in front of a long, low building. Tori didn't wait for him to turn off the engine. She was off the bike, sprinting to the clinic door, bruises and pain forgotten as she pushed the door open and stepped into the wide lobby. It was empty. Something she'd expected so late in the evening. The Raymonds' apartment was at the back of the clinic, and she headed that way, knowing a buzzer had already announced her presence. Any minute now, either Mark or Joi would come to see who'd arrived.

As if on cue, the soft pad of feet sounded in the hall and a feminine voice called out. "*Sawatdee kha.*"

"Joi? It's Tori."

"Tori!" Joi Raymond raced around the corner. "Praise God. We've been worried sick. Your grandfather called us and said you'd never arrived home. Are you…?" Her voice trailed off as she caught sight of Tori's head covering and tunic. "Tori?"

"Yes. It's me."

Joi lunged forward, pulling Tori into an embrace that threatened to crack her bruised ribs. "Where have you been?"

"It's a long story." And she didn't have time to tell it. "Are Melody and Mark in the apartment?"

"Yes. What—?"

Chet stepped into the clinic, his arrival cutting off whatever question Joi planned to ask. He spoke in Thai, the words a jumble of sounds that Tori couldn't understand. What she did understand was the expression on Joi's face—one of disbelief and worry. Before Chet finished speaking, Joi reached out and tugged the scarf from Tori's face. Her gaze touched on Tori's cheek and jaw, her fingers prodding at bruised flesh. "Who did this to you?"

"I don't know. I only know what they want. The box Melody's locket was in."

"Why?"

"I wish I knew."

"We'll figure it out together. Let's go take a look." Joi looped an arm around Tori's waist, her calm, even tone at odds with the worry in her eyes. "Chet, why don't you head home? It's getting dark and the road in is difficult at night."

"I will stay and give Tori a ride back."

"If she leaves, Mark can give her a ride." No doubt, Joi was as worried as Tori about Chet's well-being.

As they argued, Tori could almost hear the clock ticking away precious seconds. Noah might show up at any time. "It's late. I may stay the night. Go home, and if I need a ride, I'll call you."

He hesitated, then nodded. "I will pray for your safety."

As soon as he stepped out the door, Joi hurried Tori through the clinic and into the family's apartment. "Mark! Melody!"

The fact that she shouted the names told Tori exactly how shaken she was. A former E.R. doctor, Joi never panicked, her calm confidence as evident in her family life as it was in her work.

"What's up?" Mark stepped out of the den, his salt-and-pepper hair standing on end as if he'd run his hands through it again and again. He stopped short when he caught sight of Tori. "Praise God! We've been worried sick."

His words so neatly mimicked Joi's that Tori almost smiled. "I know. I'm sorry."

"From the look of things, it wasn't your fault. Sit down."

"Tori?" Melody stepped out of the hall that led to the apartment's two bedrooms, her slim frame a replica of Tori's at the same age.

"Yep, I missed you so much I had to come back." This time, Tori did smile, though she was sure it was a weak imitation of the real thing.

"What happened to your face? It looks like someone beat you up." Melody's eyes were deep green and filled with concern. At thirteen, she had her parents' compassion and need to heal.

"Just an accident. Listen, could you bring out the box I sent your locket in? The little rosewood one."

"Sure. I love the locket, by the way. Thank you so much." She grabbed Tori in a bear hug that stole her breath, then released her and ran back down the hall.

As soon as she disappeared from view, Mark placed a hand on Tori's shoulder and urged her to the couch. "Sit down. You're white as a ghost."

"I'm always white. Goes with the red hair." She sat anyway, hoping she'd be able to get up when the time came.

"Not this kind of white. The bruises on your face are obvious. Where else are you hurt?"

"Everywhere, but not serious enough to worry about now."

"Here it is." Melody hurried back into the room, waving the small rosewood box.

"Thanks." Tori accepted the box, her flesh crawling as if she were holding a snake. Two inches by two inches and less than an inch tall, it was beautifully detailed with inlaid mother-of-pearl. A tiny gold clasp and gold hinges were the only other adornments.

Tori pulled the box open, saw nothing but gleaming wood.

"See anything?" Joi leaned close.

"What are we looking for?" Mark joined his wife, sliding an arm around her shoulders and peering down at the box.

"I don't know, but whatever it is, it's important. Mind if I take this with me, Melody?"

"No. Do you need the locket, too?" Melody fingered the silver heart that hung from a chain around her neck. An exact replica of the one Tori owned, it contained a copy of her grandparents' wedding portrait. Seeing Melody wearing it brought bittersweet longing—both for the grandmother who'd taken Tori in when no one else would, and for the daughter Tori had given up.

Or maybe it was just for the things she'd lost, things she could never have again.

She forced the feelings aside, not allowing regret or discontent. Her life was what she'd made it, her choices her own. All she could do now was move forward. Wherever that might lead. "No way. That's yours. Now I've really got to go."

"What?" The words were shrill, Joi's expression one of disbelief. "And go where?"

"Away from here."

"Melody, why don't you go in your room and finish your homework?" Mark spoke to his daughter, his concerned gaze on Tori.

"It's done."

"Go anyway."

"Fine. I know when I'm not wanted." She smiled, bent to place a quick kiss on Tori's cheek.

"Goodbye, Melody." Tori kept her voice light, her grip loose as she leaned forward and stole one last hug. "I love you."

"Love you, too."

With that, Melody hurried back down the hall.

"You can't really intend to go back out there? Whatever that box is, it's too dangerous for you to carry it around with you." Joi spoke in a whisper.

"And too dangerous for me to stay here with it. The men who abducted me haven't given up. They want me and they want this box. If they trace me here, you'll all be in danger. I have to leave before that happens."

"But where will you go?" This time it was Mark who spoke, his voice calmer than Joi's had been.

"Bangkok. I'll take the box to the embassy. Someone there will know what to do with it." Tori stood up, lifted the caftan and shoved the box into the pocket of her jeans.

Mark put a hand on her arm, holding her in place when she would have shoved open the apartment door. "Wait. Let's take a few minutes. Think things through, decide if you going to Bangkok is the best idea. Then if you still want to leave, I'll drive you to town."

She didn't plan to let him drive her anywhere, but she nodded anyway, turning to face the couple who'd offered her both friendship and advice in the years since they'd adopted Melody. "Thinking things through is fine, but it won't help. We still won't know what the box is, who wants it or why."

"We don't have to know any of that." Joi paced across the room, her short, compact body almost vibrating with energy as she reached for the phone. "Now let's pray we've got a good connection."

"Who are you calling?"

"The U.S. Embassy. Maybe they can send someone to escort you to Bangkok or give you the name of someone in Mae Hong Son who can help."

Tori nodded, surprised that she hadn't thought of that herself. But then, she wasn't just running scared, she was running on empty, all of her energy drained, her body pulsing with pain.

"It's ringing. Here." Joi handed the phone to Tori.

She pressed it to her ear, her heart thundering as a woman's cheerful voice filled the line. "United States Embassy. How may I direct your call?"

Good question. "I..."

"Yes?"

"I'm an American citizen and I've run into trouble up-country. I'm hoping someone there can help me."

"Do you need legal representation?"

"No. At least I don't think I do."

"If you give me your name, a number where you can be reached, and tell me what kind of trouble you're in, I can pass the information to the right party."

"Thank you. My name is Tori Riley. I—"

"Is that Victoria Riley?" The cheerful good humor had dropped away.

"Yes."

"Please hold. I'm transferring your call."

"To whom?" But she'd already been put on hold, the soft rhythm of a love song playing across the line.

"Hello? Ms. Riley?" This time it was a man, his voice smooth and soothing.

"Yes."

"Jack McKenzie. What can I do for you?"

"I'm not sure."

"Then tell me what the trouble is, and I'll see if I can figure something out."

"I bought a box at a *wat* near Mae Hong Son. I don't know what it is, but a lot of people are after it."

"Where's the box now?"

"I have it. I'd like to bring it to the embassy and let someone there take a look at it."

"Sounds like a good plan."

"I don't know how long it will take me to get there. I'm going to—"

"Stay put. An escort is on the way."

"I can't wait." Not with so many people searching for her. And not when discovery could mean death, both hers and the Raymonds'.

"You won't need to. He's there."

As if on cue, a loud buzz announced that someone had entered the clinic. Tori's mouth went dry with fear and she knew her eyes were as wide, her skin as pale, as Joi's.

"Stay here. I'll go see who it is."

"No!" Tori and Joi spoke in unison, but Mark was already pushing the door open and stepping out of the apartment.

"Everything okay?" Jack McKenzie's voice pulled Tori back to their conversation.

"Yes." She hoped.

"Good. My man will escort you to my office in Chiang Mai. We'll see what's what, and have you home before you know it."

Home. The word sounded too good to be true, but before she could say as much, the apartment door swung open and Mark stepped back inside, another man on his heels. Tall, pitch-black hair, and eyes the blue-green of the ocean, Noah moved into the room with the same pantherlike grace Tori had noticed when he'd freed her. His gaze scanned the room coming to rest on Tori as he slid a dark backpack from his shoulder.

"Guess we meet again, Red."

Tori could think of nothing nice to say, so she said nothing at all, holding the phone to her ear, her fingers in a death grip around the receiver as Mark introduced Noah and Joi to one another.

"That Jack?" Noah gestured to the phone.

"Yes."

"Mind if I speak to him?" His hand slipped around hers, sliding over tense fingers and somehow easing her grip before she realized what he was doing. Then her hand was empty and he was speaking into the phone.

"Jack? Yeah. The clinic. Maybe twenty miles outside the city. Right. I was thinking the same." He paused, met Tori's eyes. "You have the box?"

She considered denying it, but there was no reason now. Noah was on her side. Or was supposed to be. She still wasn't sure she trusted him. She pulled the box from her pocket anyway, handing it to Noah before she could rethink her decision.

He met her gaze as he turned the box over, his eyes

dark and unreadable. Then he turned his attention to the mother-of-pearl inlay, pulling a small magnifying glass from his pocket and using it to examine one area after another.

Tori half expected him to say there'd been a mistake, that the box was exactly what she'd thought it to be. He didn't. Instead he paused, looked more closely at one section, and spoke into the phone. "I've got it. You sending the helo? We'll be at Mae Hong Son Airport in an hour. Yeah. I agree. I've already got it covered. I'll tell them."

He hung up the phone, swept a gaze around the room. "Anyone else here?"

"Our daughter." Joi sounded calm, but Tori sensed tension in the words. Like any good mother, she was ready to protect her child.

"You'll need to get her. Pack a few things. We're leaving here in ten minutes."

"What? We can't leave the clinic."

This time it was Mark, the disbelief in his voice obvious.

"I wish it weren't necessary, but it is."

"Maybe you should explain."

"This box was carried across the border from Myanmar and delivered with a truckload of tourist trade items. It's different than most trade items, though. It's inscribed, and it wasn't meant for sale."

"I didn't see an inscription." Tori leaned closer, caught the scent of Noah's shampoo and backed away.

"You wouldn't have. Not unless you knew where and how to look. Each letter of the inscription is the size of a red blood cell. Thirty lines of text can fit in an area the width of a strand of hair. Even with a magnifying glass it's difficult to see that there's any writing there."

"I've never heard of such a thing." Mark leaned closer, his gaze on the box, his curiosity evident.

"Most people haven't."

"Then what's the point?" Tori wanted to grab the box and the magnifying glass and look for herself.

"That is the point. The technology is new, but effective. A much more secure mode for transferring information than cell phone or computer."

"Information?"

"Dates. Times. Places of delivery. The Wa has put technology to good use."

"The Wa? Then we're talking drug trade. I'll get Melody and start packing. Mark, you want to call Dr. Graw and see if he can stay at the clinic for a while, maybe scrounge up some extra hands from Bangkok or Chiang Mai?"

"Yeah. How long are we talking, Mr. Stone?"

"Noah. I wish I could tell you."

Mark looked like he'd press for more, but seemed to think better of it. Instead, he gave Joi's shoulder a quick, comforting squeeze. "I'll use the phone in the clinic and make sure things are locked up while I'm there."

He hurried away and Joi followed suit, heading down the hall to find Melody.

Which left Tori alone with Noah and the bitter knowledge that her visit to Thailand had led to the destruction of the safe, fulfilling life her friends had worked so hard to create.

Chapter Five

"Your friends are better off away from here." Noah spoke as he slipped the box inside his pack.

"I know." Pale, drawn, dark bruises standing out in stark relief against her skin, Tori's voice betrayed none of what she felt. It was her eyes that spoke volumes, and Noah had read every bit of the story they told as she watched her friends walk out of the room.

"Then why do you look like you think their lives are about to end?" He slipped the pack back on and met her gaze head-on.

"Because they are. At least their lives as they know them."

"For a while maybe."

"Longer than that. Do you really think they'll be able to return here? That they won't be targets of revenge because of what I've done?"

"What have you done?"

Her face hardened, her eyes flashing fire. "This is no confession, if that's what you're looking for."

"I'm looking for the truth."

"The truth is exactly what I told you before. I bought that box as a gift for Melody. I didn't know about the information on it. I didn't know that I was getting in the way of the Wa's plans. But I don't think that's going to matter to them. What will matter is that I caused them trouble. What better way to get back at me than to hurt the people I care about?"

"It's not the Wa you have to worry about. It's Sang Lao."

"You mentioned him before. The name isn't any more familiar to me now than it was then."

"He's a local businessman. The Thai Royal Police and the DEA have suspected him of drug running for years. They just haven't been able to prove it. The information on the box might be just what they need to put him in jail and throw away the key."

"And if it is? Will the Raymonds be safe here? Or will there still be retribution because they helped me?"

"We're ready." Joi's entrance into the room saved Noah from having to answer. The girl at her side had Tori's long, lean frame and deep red hair. Though her face was heart-shaped rather than oval, her eyes startling green rather than chocolate-brown, there was no mistaking the connection between birth mother and daughter.

"You have enough packed for a couple days?"

Noah wondered if he was the only one that heard the break in Tori's voice as she asked the question.

Joi held up two large duffels. "Plenty. And I had Melody grab an extra pair of jeans and a T-shirt for you, Tori."

"Thanks."

"I've got a medical kit, too. Once we get wherever

we're going, we'll get some of those cuts and bruises fixed up."

Unfortunately they weren't going to the same place. But that was something Noah thought would be better discussed when they were safely away from the clinic. "Let's head out."

Mark was still on the phone when they entered the clinic lobby. He gestured for another minute, said a few more words and hung up. "Everything's set. Dr. Graw's going to stay here until we get back. Let me just run through, make sure everything is locked up. Then we're out of here."

Noah forced back impatience as Mark checked the clinic one last time. He understood the doctor's need to make sure things were secure, but he could feel the hot breath of danger on his neck and the skin-crawling awareness that said trouble was coming and coming fast.

"Almost done?"

Mark turned from the window he was about to double-check and must have caught something in Noah's gaze, because he let his arms drop to his sides and nodded. "We're set."

"We should pray before we go." Joi put a hand on her husband's arm, her bright blue gaze moving from one person to the next.

"There's no time for that, Joi. We've got to get moving." Tori started toward the door, not quite hiding a grimace of pain as she moved.

Noah caught the back of the caftan she wore. "There's always time to pray."

It was a truth he lived by, though from the expression on Tori's face she didn't believe it. He thought she might argue, but then her gaze went to Melody who stood wide-eyed and curious next to her mother. "Right. You're right. Let's pray."

"Noah? Would you mind?" Mark moved into place beside Melody, offering one hand to his daughter and the other to Noah.

"Sure." He linked hands with Mark, then reached for Tori, felt her fingers curl around his, and wondered what her life had been like before she'd come to Thailand.

He bowed his head, stilled his thoughts and offered a quick prayer for God's protection and guidance. When he finished, he met Tori's eyes. "Ready?"

"As ready as I'll ever be."

"Good. I'll go first. See if it's clear. Our ride is waiting half a mile down the road." With that, he pushed open the door and stepped outside. The jungle hissed and howled, alive with night sounds, the darkness deep and impenetrable beyond the pale glow of clinic light.

Noah whistled once. High and piercing. Simon answered immediately—a long, low response that carried on the balmy night air.

Satisfied, Noah called into the still-open door, "We're good. Let's go."

Tori came first, moving quickly, as if facing her terror were the only way to conquer it. The Raymonds followed, Mark and Joi flanking their daughter, offering protection in the only way they could. Darkness made the going hazardous, deep ruts and low-hanging branches a danger to unwary travelers. Noah set the pace at a brisk walk rather than the full-out run he would have preferred. Even so, he could hear the quiet pant of Tori's breath, the stuttering stumble of hesitant feet. He wanted to slow down but didn't dare.

By the time they reached the sedan, his nerves were on edge, the heavy weight of his gun a slick, cool comfort in his hand.

Simon paced the area in front of the car, tension and energy flowing off him in waves. "We need to get moving. I don't like the way things feel."

"Me, neither." Noah yanked the back door open, hurrying Mark, Joi and Melody inside.

Tori was next and he pulled open the front door. "Climb in."

"Maybe I should—"

"We don't have time to discuss your options. Get in." His voice was hard, as he'd intended.

She scooted inside and he followed, his thigh and shoulder brushing Tori's as he closed the door.

She shifted away, her body rigid.

"Move any farther and you'll be in the driver's seat."

"There's not enough room for three people up here."

Simon slid into the driver's seat, crowding her even more, and Noah had the feeling she wanted to climb across his lap and out the door.

He leaned toward her, inhaling the scent of jasmine and fear, wondering at her obvious discomfort around men. Had she been hurt before? Abused in some way? "Relax."

"I don't like small spaces. Maybe we should switch. I'll sit near the window."

"Sorry. People with guns get the window seats."

"Oh." The sum total of her response. Tori lifted a hand and wiped a bead of sweat from her forehead. She wasn't lying about close spaces. She'd been claustrophobic for years, thanks to her stepfather. But that wasn't the only thing bothering her. The man sitting beside her was adding a lot to the problem. Funny, Noah's friend was just as tall, just as broad-shouldered, and didn't seem to take up nearly the room Noah did.

Tori shifted again, trying to put some distance between her leg and Noah's. All she managed to do was elbow the man driving. "Sorry."

He grunted by way of response, his gaze never wavering from the twisting road in front of them. The air in the car felt heavy and warm, the caftan Tori wore a suffocating blanket against her skin. The fabric brushed against the raw wounds on her wrists, irritating the sensitive skin there. She tried to push up the sleeves, but they were too full, and fell back into place within seconds. Maybe taking the caftan off would be the best idea. She leaned forward, grabbed the hem.

"Sit still already." Noah's friend barked the words and Tori froze.

"No need to snap her head off, Simon." The words were quiet, smooth, with just a hint of warning.

"No need for her to wiggle like a worm on a hook, either."

Tori planned to apologize, but before she could form the words, Noah spoke again.

"We're all tense. Worst thing we can do is take that out on each other."

"Right, but I still think she should sit still."

Tori ignored the remark, straightening her spine and trying to force her mind away from the close confines, the heat and the pain that pulsed through her each time the car bounced over a rut. But what else was there to think about but danger, uncertainty and fear?

"Everything's going to be okay." Noah whispered the words in her ear, his breath a warm caress against her cheek, his arm slipping around her shoulder, urging her closer.

She knew she should protest, but the weight of his arm was comforting, the rhythm of his breathing a strange lullaby to her fatigue-numbed mind. "I wish I could believe that."

"It's not about believing. It's about faith."

"Faith in what? God's ability to get us all out of this mess?"

"In God's ability to bring something good out of whatever happens."

"Even if that means one of us doesn't make it?"

"Even then."

Not according to Tori. She couldn't imagine any good coming from the death of one of the Raymonds. Or from her own death, for that matter. Nor could she imagine anything good coming from Noah lying bleeding and broken on the ground. She shuddered and forced the image from her mind.

In the backseat, Joi and Mark murmured to one another, their words a quiet litany that rose and fell in waves. Even the softness of their voices couldn't hide the affection they had for one another. Respect and joint history knit them together, love held them there. When she'd chosen them to parent Melody, Tori had known they had the kind of marriage that would weather life's storms. At the time, she'd dreamed of having the same one day. She'd been young, foolish and still able to dream. Now all her dreams were nightmares, and she'd decided the best thing she could do for herself was forget that she'd once wanted marriage, kids. Love.

Her eyes drifted closed, her head nodding forward.

She jerked upright, felt Noah's hand press against her cheek, urging her toward him again. "Relax."

"I—"

"We've got a long night ahead of us. Why not rest now, while you have the chance?"

Because she didn't want to rest, didn't want to give up control even for a few minutes. She especially didn't want to lean on a man who'd used her to further his own cause, no matter that the cause was a noble one.

But somehow her head found its way to Noah's shoulder, her body relaxed against his, soothed by the quiet hum of voices, the gentle bump and sway of the car. She closed her eyes, telling herself it was only for a minute, and drifted off to sleep.

Noah didn't want to wake Tori and wished there was some way to get out of the car without doing so. Unfortunately, her head lay heavy against his shoulder, her hand fisted in a handful of his shirt as if she'd been afraid of being abandoned while she slept. The only way to get out of the car was to move her.

"Wake up, Red."

The words were quiet. Her reaction anything but. She jerked awake, arms flailing out, a scream dying just before it took wing.

"Hey, calm down."

She blinked, her eyes dark pools in the dim glow of the car's interior light. "What's going on?"

"We're at the safe house."

She turned, saw the empty backseat. "Safe house? Where are the Raymonds?"

"They're already inside."

"I thought we were going to Chiang Mai."

"We are, but there isn't room in the chopper for everyone. The Raymonds will stay here until Jack arranges an escort to Chiang Mai for them."

"What? Why didn't you tell me this before?"

"Didn't want to waste time arguing over something that couldn't be changed."

"I want to see them." She scrambled for the door, pushing it open and stepping out into the night, almost stumbling in her haste to get to the house.

"Slow down. You're going to break your neck." He grabbed her arm, forcing her to slow her pace as they approached the hulking building. Her bones felt fragile beneath his hand, her muscles smooth and strong. Not a woman to sit idle, but one who'd want to be out doing, seeing, experiencing. Even now she was tugging against his hold, hurrying toward Hawke's fortress, not content to stroll when she could run.

Built on top of a steep hill, the house was a dark shadow jutting toward the sky. Closed-circuit cameras lined the ten-foot fence that enclosed the yard. Noah counted five, but knew there were more. The Raymonds would be safe here, that much he knew. All he had to do was convince Tori of the fact.

"Victoria Holt."

"What?" Noah glanced at Tori, saw that her gaze was focused on the house.

"This house is the perfect setting for a Victoria Holt novel. Dark, brooding. All it needs is a tragic hero. One with a scar and a mysterious past."

It had one, but Noah would let her figure that out herself.

He rapped on the front door and stepped back while it swung in.

Tori gasped, then tried to cover the sound with a cough. The man who stood in the doorway stared her down, his face set in a scowl, the scar that sliced across his cheek tugging down the corner of his mouth and adding menace to his already-unfriendly appearance.

"Tori Riley, Hawke Morran."

"Nice to meet you, Mr. Morran."

"I doubt it. And it's Hawke."

"I—"

"You've got a ride to meet, and your friends are waiting to say goodbye. They're in the first room on the left."

Dismissed. Just like that. Tori shrugged off the urge to ignore his subtle command and hurried down the hall. The Raymonds were sitting on a long sofa, coffee and sodas set on the table in front of them. They stood as Tori entered the room, Joi and Mark hurrying toward her. Melody hung back, allowing the adults a moment to talk.

Tori motioned her over. "I've only got a minute. Come say goodbye."

"I'm sorry all this happened, Tori."

"Why should you be sorry? You didn't do anything wrong."

"I asked you to come for my birthday. If I hadn't—"

"I would have come anyway, so stop worrying and give me a hug."

Melody complied, her thin, strong arms wrapping around Tori's waist. "Be careful."

"You be careful, too." She released her hold and turned toward Joi, not wanting Melody to see the moisture in her eyes. "Noah said the DEA is sending people to escort you to Chiang Mai. It shouldn't be long."

"He explained what's going on. We'll be fine, so don't waste any energy worrying about us. Concentrate on being careful and keeping safe."

"I will." But she'd still worry.

Joi must have seen the truth in her eyes. "Everything will be okay. You'll see."

"I hope you're right."

"I am." She hugged Tori, the gesture more gentle than Melody's. "I'll be praying for you."

"I'll be praying for you, too." And she would, even though she thought the chances were slim that God would listen.

"Why don't I come with you?" There were new lines on Mark's face, worry aging him as life had not.

"I wish there were room on the helicopter to bring you, but there isn't." Noah stepped into the room, his gaze on Tori. "We need to get moving."

She knew they did, but hesitated anyway, her skin crawling with nerves at the thought of leaving the house. Beyond the gated yard and well-protected walls, men were searching for her, men who wouldn't hesitate to hurt or kill. She'd experienced their cruelty firsthand and had no desire to do so again.

She forced herself to say goodbye to the Raymonds and follow Noah out of the room.

Hawke stood in the hall, watching Tori through cool gray eyes as she moved past. Even without the scowl and the scar, he'd look formidable. Even deadly. Hopefully that meant the Raymonds were safe in his care.

"Jack says he'll have men here before noon tomorrow." Noah spoke as he pulled open the door, his words directed at Hawke, though Tori thought the reassurance might also be for her.

"He'd better. I've got business in Bangkok tomorrow night."

"Jack's a man of his word."

"Guess we'll see. You taking my brother to Chiang Mai?"

"You think he'll want to visit the DEA?"

"Maybe. For the right reason."

"Wish I could bring him, then, but the DEA's sending a retired gunner. No room for another passenger."

"Thought that was a two-man helo."

"It is. We'll make do."

Hawke shrugged, turning his attention to Tori. "Shouldn't be too hard to squeeze her in."

She shifted under his gaze, but refused to look away. "Like Noah said, we'll make do. Thank you for looking out for my friends while we're gone."

"I'm not doing it for you."

She bit back a rude response, waiting for him to say more.

He didn't. It was Noah who broke the silence, putting a hand on Tori's elbow and urging her out the front door. "You know where to reach me if there's trouble."

"Right." Hawke didn't bother with goodbye, just waited until they cleared the threshold and then shut the door firmly behind them.

The soft glow of outside lights did little to chase away the darkness or the mist that hovered over the ground. Tori shivered, her gaze traveling the parameters of the yard, searching for a danger she knew she wouldn't see. At least not until it was too late.

Up ahead, Simon stood near the sedan, his tall, lean frame still and alert. Perhaps he sensed danger in the deepening shadows. He wasn't the only one. Noah's hand tightened on Tori's elbow, and he urged her to move more quickly. She complied, hurrying to the sedan and sliding into the backseat. Simon and Noah took the front, leaving her with plenty of room to move and breathe. It didn't help. Instead of feeling relief, she felt alone, defenseless, an easy mark.

"You okay back there?"

"Yes."

But she wasn't. She wanted to get out of the car, run back into the house and the illusion of safety it offered. She wanted to skip the trip to Chiang Mai and head straight for Bangkok International and a flight home. But more than anything, she wanted to believe Noah's assurance that everything was going to be okay, that somehow God would work things out for good, no matter what the outcome of the next few hours.

She wanted to believe it, but she couldn't.

Instead she'd just have to wait things out, be ready for whatever would come, and hope that whatever it was wouldn't destroy her or the Raymonds.

Chapter Six

Mae Hong Son Airport boasted one runway and one building. Quiet and laid-back by any standard, it accepted thrice-daily arrivals and departures with cheerful ease. Tori had been there twice, both times during the day when bright sunlight reflected off the tarmac, and the surrounding jungles and mountains shimmered with mist. Now, with deep blackness shrouding the landscape, the airport seemed a desolate place.

"You sure you're expected?" Simon pulled the car up in front of the darkened entrance.

"We're expected."

Hopefully by no one but the DEA and airport employees.

Tori didn't share her worries. Just waited while Noah and Simon stepped out of the car. Their gazes swept the nearly empty parking lot, the deep hedge of bushes that lined the walk and the low-slung building that housed a ticket counter and waiting area. Safe in the dark confines of the sedan, Tori felt like a well-guarded politician. Or a high-profile criminal. She shook her head against the thought. The last thing she needed to worry about was whether or not the DEA would believe her story. But worry was something she excelled at. Images of herself, dressed in prison garb and speaking to Pops through bulletproof glass, filled her mind.

The door opened and Simon leaned into the car. "When the guard opens the door, we move. Straight to the building. Stay in front of me. If I tell you to drop, you drop. Got it?"

"Yes." She glanced past him and saw Noah rapping at the airport's glass door, his back to the parking lot and to any danger that might lurk in the darkness beyond.

"Don't worry. It's not him they're after."

"That doesn't mean they won't hurt him."

"You're right, but they'll wait until you're out of the car to strike. Try to cut Stone and me down, then come in for you. If that happens, stay low and get into the airport. Close the door. Find a place to hide. Don't come out until the DEA arrives." The words were matter of fact, as if danger were part of his everyday life. And maybe it was.

Tori met Simon's cold stare and wondered who he was, how he was connected to Noah and what Noah had done to win such loyal friendship from two men who obviously had little love for their fellow man. The look in Simon's eyes was enough to keep her from asking the questions. Instead, she waited, silent and tense, counting the seconds until the airport door opened.

After what seemed an eternity, a tall, rangy guard peered out, his face a pale oval in the darkness. He spoke to Noah, though Tori couldn't hear the words, and Noah responded, speaking in smooth Thai.

"This is it. Ready?" Simon leaned in, holding out a hand.

Tori grasped it, feeling the cool dryness of his palm. Hers was damp with nerves and she was sure he noticed. She lifted her chin, looked him in the eye. "Ready."

"Let's move." Noah's voice whipped across the parking lot, and Simon yanked Tori out of the car. She stumbled, righted herself and started toward the building, Simon so close behind that she could feel the heat of his body against her back. Her heart crashed sickeningly in her chest, her eyes searching every shadow for danger. She expected to hear gunfire, the sound of a body thudding onto the pavement. But she heard nothing except the quiet gasp of her breath as she struggled to control her panic.

Noah faced the parking lot now, a gun in his hand. He looked deadly, intent on doing whatever it took to get Tori to the DEA's headquarters.

"Inside." He barked the command as she reached the portico that sheltered the door.

She ran past him, her feet slipping on the tiled floor in the lobby. Simon clapped a hand on her shoulder, keeping her from falling. "Keep moving. We're just as much sitting ducks inside as we are outside if we stay near these doors and windows."

She glanced around, desperate to be away from the door, but not sure which way to run.

"The hallway." Irritation and frustration seeped from Simon's voice.

Tori hurried across the lobby and into the dimly lit corridor, Simon still behind her, his footsteps silent, a prickling at the nape of her neck her only clue that he was still there.

"Stay here." He pushed her against the wall and moved back down the hall, disappearing into the shadows so quickly Tori wasn't sure if he'd really gone.

Nothing moved. No sound broke the silence. She waited, her pulse slowing, adrenaline fading. What was taking so long? Would she hear a shot if one was fired? Or were they using silencers?

"We're clear."

She jumped, turned to face Noah, her hands clasped to her stomach to still their trembling. "You scared me half to death."

"Sorry. I came in a back door. Things look clear outside. No sign of Lao's men." He sounded distracted, worried, and that worried Tori.

"Isn't that a good thing?"

"Yeah, it is."

"Then why do you sound worried?"

"Not worried. Cautious. Come on. The chopper's ten minutes out. We'll wait in the guard's office while Simon stands watch."

"Will he?" The doubt in her voice was clear as Tori fell into step beside Noah, moving with him down the hall.

"He may not want to be here, but he'll stay. He's loyal to his brother, and Hawke's loyal to me."

"Hawke doesn't seem like the kind who's loyal to anyone."

"Maybe not, but I saved his life a few years back and he hasn't forgotten it."

Tori cast a dubious look his way.

Noah sighed and pushed open a door at the far end of the hall. "Anyone ever tell you you're too young to be so cynical?"

"I'm not that young."

"So you're not denying the cynical part?"

"I don't call it cynicism. I call it realism."

"Means the same thing. Go ahead and sit down." He

gestured to a plastic chair that sat against one wall and Tori eased down onto the hard seat.

"What happens when we get to Chiang Mai?"

"I'll pass the box on to Jack. He'll ask you a few questions. If things go well, you'll be on a plane home by tomorrow night."

"And if they don't?"

"Then it might be a while longer before you get on that plane."

"How much longer?" A day? A week? More?

Noah shrugged and pulled a second chair out from behind a metal desk. "As long as it takes for Jack to be satisfied that he's got the whole story."

"He already has the whole story. At least my end of it." The words had a weary edge that Noah couldn't ignore. He shifted to face Tori, caught the look of frustration that flashed across her face.

He wanted to offer her encouragement, assure her that she'd be on a plane home within hours, but he wouldn't tell her less than the truth. "Jack won't keep you any longer than necessary."

"I've already been in Thailand longer than I'd planned. My grandfather was expecting me home five days ago. I've got to be back at work and..."

"And what?"

"I'm ready to go home. Funny, a few weeks ago I thought I'd be happy to never go back." Her smile didn't reach her eyes.

"Never? That's a long time."

"And yet, still not long enough for Lakeview residents to forget my latest romance debacle." There was wry humor in the tone, and beneath it the hard edge of frustration.

"Should I ask?"

"Why not? Everyone at home does." She ran a hand over her hair, sighed deeply. "My fiancé, Kyle, was a lot more interested in my inheritance than he was in me. I found out the hard way—caught him going through some papers in my grandfather's office one Sunday after church."

"Maybe—"

"Maybe nothing. When I asked him what he was doing he said that my grandfather was getting older, that if Pops didn't have a will, his assets might become property of the state, or some long-lost relative might come forward and demand his portion. I told Kyle I didn't care what happened to Pops' property when he was gone."

"What'd he think about that?"

"He wanted me to ask about the will. I refused. He insisted. That's when I decided we weren't right for each other."

"Good thinking."

"I thought so, but a lot of the ladies in Lakeview think I'm going to become an old maid. They want me married with kids. The sooner, the better. So, a year after my broken engagement, they're still asking me if I'm okay and trying to fix me up with brothers, uncles and good friends." She said it with aplomb, but Noah could see the hurt in her eyes.

"Someone needs to have a talk with that former fiancé of yours."

"Pops blistered his ear and probably would have blackened his eye if I'd let him."

"Pops sounds like my kind of guy."

"He's everyone's kind of guy. Just an all-around good person. I hope he's okay."

"We'll call when we get to Chiang Mai. You can let him know you're all right."

"If he's not already on his way here."

"He's not. He's got a flight out day after tomorrow."

"I won't ask you how you know that." She leaned her head back against the wall and smiled. A real smile this time. One that added a tinge of color to her pale cheeks and softened the stubborn line of her chin. Beneath her swollen bruises, there was beauty in the angles and planes of her face, the kind that would only multiply with age. Noah could picture her forty years from now, still tall, still slim, her face lined with life and with laughter.

Not a good thing to be imagining when Tori was still a suspected drug runner.

He pulled his thoughts up short. "Your grandfather loves you a lot. He's been calling the embassy every hour for three days."

"Pops is something else. Seventy-six years old and still running to my rescue."

"You need a lot of rescuing?"

"Not anymore, but Pops hasn't figured that out yet. I just hope he's not so worried he forgets to take care of himself." Her smile faded as quickly as it had come, worry for her grandfather stealing whatever momentary peace she'd found.

Noah resisted the urge to lay his hand over hers, to offer comfort and reassurance. Tori didn't seem the kind who'd want either. "What are you worried about?"

"I'm worried he'll get on that plane and come here. That like any good and decent knight, he'll rush to the rescue without any regard for his own well-being. I'm worried he'll be hurt because of me."

"If he's hurt, it won't be because of you."

"Maybe not, but I still don't want him here. It's too dangerous. Not that there'll be any stopping him. He won't be content until he sees for himself that I'm okay."

"'An all-around good person.'" He repeated the words Tori had used, but she didn't seem to notice.

"He is. I can't wait to see him again." The longing in her voice was unmistakable.

Noah understood it, the desire for family and home something he'd known too well during his years in Thailand. "You'll be back with your grandfather soon, Red. I'll make sure of it."

"Will you?"

"Yeah. I will. Come on. I hear the helicopter."

Tori didn't hear anything, but allowed Noah to pull her to her feet. His hand was firm and warm around hers, the rough calluses on his palm rasping against her skin. He didn't release his grip as he walked to the door, the feel of his hand wrapped around hers strangely intimate.

How long had it been since a man had held her hand? Kyle never had. Nor had Joe. Melody's father might have, but it was so long ago, Tori couldn't remember.

How long had it been since she had *wanted* a man to hold her hand? Had she ever? Probably not. Men weren't to be trusted. People in general weren't to be trusted.

She glanced at Noah, wondering what kind of person he was, wondering when he'd show his true colors. Whatever they might be. "Have you been with the DEA long?"

"Ten years before I retired."

"Retired?"

"I'm here as a favor to Jack."

"Coming here seems like an awfully big favor."

"Not so big. I know the area and the people here. That makes getting information easier than it might be for someone else. Besides, I'm as anxious to close Lao down as Jack. Come on, through here."

He pushed open a door and stepped outside, putting a hand on Tori's arm to hold her in place. She could hear the rumbling thud of rotor blades beating the night air. Her own nerves jumped, adrenaline pulsing through her. She'd never flown in a helicopter before. But then, she'd never been kidnapped, tortured, or pursued by drug traffickers before, either.

"You ever ride in a helicopter before?" Noah shouted the words above the thunderous beat of the rotors.

"There's a first time for everything."

"As firsts go, this shouldn't be too bad."

The chopper touched down, churning the air and whipping dust and debris into frenzied motion. Soon it would lift off again, carrying Noah and Tori to Chiang Mai. The knowledge should have brought relief. Instead, Noah couldn't shake the feeling that something was wrong. He glanced around, saw nothing that triggered an alarm, felt nothing out of the ordinary.

"Let's go." He urged Tori toward the helicopter, his nerves alive with warning, his mind shouting that Lao should have made a move by now, that if he hadn't, there was a reason. A big one.

What? Noah scrambled for an answer as he helped Tori up into the helicopter.

Chase Murray sat at the controls, his easy grin flashing in Tori's direction before he turned his attention to Noah.

"Good to see you again, Noah." The shouted words were barely audible above the helicopter's thundering blades.

"You, too. Wish it were under different circumstances, though."

"That makes two of us. Passenger's going to have to sit in the cargo area. She'll fit better than you."

"Can you manage, Tori?"

But she was already moving into the small area behind the seats, wincing a little as she maneuvered into the space meant for supplies and weapons. "I'm fine."

She didn't look fine. She looked crowded and uncomfortable, deep hollows beneath her eyes and cheekbones adding gauntness to her already-thin, bruised face. Since there was nothing that could be done about it, Noah handed her a headset and motioned for her to put it on. Then he settled into the seat beside Chase and slid his own headset on.

"Sorry about this, ma'am. Best we could do on such short notice." Chase's tinny voice sounded through the speakers.

"I'll be okay." There was a breathless quality to Tori's voice, and Noah turned to meet her eyes.

"You sure?"

"Do I have a choice?"

"No."

"Then I'm sure."

"That's the spirit, ma'am." The grin in Chase's voice was obvious, and Noah could see an answering smile on Tori's lips. That he wished the smile were directed his way was a surprise. He knew better than to allow himself the luxury of personal involvement. He was here to do a job. The best thing he could do for Tori and for himself was to keep that in mind.

"How long will it take to reach Chiang Mai?" Tori's voice interrupted his thoughts, and Noah glanced at Chase, letting him answer.

"Forty-five minutes. Should be an easy trip."

Should be, but that didn't mean it would be. Sang Lao couldn't let Tori go so easily. Smart, savvy and cautious, Lao had eluded the DEA for years. Now his business, his family and his life were on the line. The Thai government didn't go easy on men who trafficked in heroin. Nor would the Wa forgive the loss of the millions of dollars in revenue the information on the box would ensure.

So why hadn't Lao made a move yet? No way he didn't know Tori was in Mae Hong Son. No way he hadn't learned of the Raymonds. By all rights, he should have attacked at the clinic, or tried to intercept Simon's car on the way to the airport. He hadn't, and that worried Noah. A lot.

"We set?" Chase met his eyes.

"Yeah."

"Then let's do it."

The chopper lurched and Tori gasped, the sound cut off as if she'd forced it back. Noah shifted in his seat, angling his body so he could see her. She looked tense, drawn and more alone than anyone should be. He reached for her hand, easing open her fingers, massaging the deep crescents gouged into her skin. "Don't worry. Chase is the best pilot I know."

"How many do you know?"

"A few."

"That's comforting."

Chase laughed, his deep rumble matching the pulsing thud of the chopper blades. "I'll get you there. You can count on it."

"Thanks." Her eyes were on Noah as she spoke, and he knew what she was thinking—that getting to Chiang Mai in one piece was the least of her worries. She didn't say as much, just let her lips curve into a half smile as she tugged her hand from his.

If he could have told her that the worst was behind them, he would have. But he couldn't, not when his gut was telling him that trouble was coming fast. "Chase hasn't lost a passenger yet."

"Good. I want to make it back home. My adventures here will be the hottest topic since Marsha Wilson decided to paint her house pink." The words were light, but Tori's hands were fisted again, her voice tight with anxiety.

"You'll get there, and Marsha's pink house will have nothing on you. You'll be the talk of the town for years."

"Longer if I end up in jail for drug trafficking."

If she'd wanted assurance that she'd be freed, that the DEA wouldn't press charges, Noah couldn't give it. Jack and his team would listen to her story, compare what she told them with what their informants were saying, compile the evidence. When it was over, they'd have a clear picture of Tori's involvement. Noah would stay with Tori until then. Make sure that the trouble he sensed was nothing more than too little sleep and too little food playing tricks on his mind.

Even as he thought it, Noah knew that his worries were brought on by much more than that. Lao hadn't given up. He wanted the box. DEA involvement or not, he planned to get it. And Noah had every intention of being near Tori when that happened.

Chapter Seven

The whitewashed room Tori sat in was beginning to feel claustrophobic. She fiddled with the half-full Coke bottle on the table in front of her and wondered what was taking so long. Two hours seemed like plenty of time to decide her fate. That's how long it had been since Noah and Jack McKenzie had left her there, and they still hadn't returned.

She glanced at the door, wishing it open, and let out a sigh of frustration when it remained closed. "What's taking so long?" She directed the question to the ice-eyed man who faced her across the table.

"Just the way things work around here." His answer was more a growl than conversation, the scowl he wore telling Tori he was as unhappy with the situation as she was. She didn't blame him. He probably thought she was a criminal, deserving of whatever fate Jack meted out and blamed her for his long wait.

"Could you go find someone? Ask what's going on?"

"'Fraid not."

Tori didn't bother arguing. They'd had the same conversation several times already. Always with the same result. She lifted the bottle, more for something to do than for a drink. She'd gulped down the first half so fast, she'd barely had time to register the sweet, syrupy taste. Now her stomach rebelled, growling a protest at too much, too soon.

It didn't help that the man had been glaring at her for most of the time that she'd been cloistered in the room. Maybe Jack thought that if he left her with Iceman long enough, she'd confess. And she might have. If she'd done something wrong. She hadn't and had no intention of waiting another few hours while Jack came to that conclusion himself. She needed to find a way out of the room. Then she'd track McKenzie down and present her side of the story.

Unless Noah had already done that for her.

The thought weaseled its way into her mind.

She pushed it aside.

She didn't need Noah to get her out of the mess she was in. She'd been taking care of herself and making her own decisions since she was fifteen. It had been difficult at first, terrifying really, but getting kicked out of her stepfather's home had served a purpose—it had made her strong. In the three months it had taken for Pops and Gran to track her down, she'd learned what it meant to go it alone. She hadn't forgotten the lesson. Nor had she ever again allowed herself to depend on someone else.

She pushed away from the table. "Where's the restroom?"

"Behind you."

Too bad. She'd been hoping that she'd have to go into the corridor to access it. "Thanks."

She pulled open the door, eager to be out of the room and away from Iceman's hard glare.

The bathroom was utilitarian and small, no window and no door besides the one she'd just walked through. She glanced up, eyeing the drop ceiling, wondering what the odds were she'd be able to push up one of the tiles and squeeze into the space between the ceiling and the floor above. Probably pretty good. As a preteen and teen she'd been locked into her room, into closets, into the attic, basement and even an old storage shed behind her stepfather's house. It had been an effective form of punishment. For a while. Then she'd learned to be creative, to look for the most unlikely means of escape and use it.

She closed the lid of the toilet and stepped onto it, pushing her hands up against the tile, sliding it to the side. There was a six-inch gap between the ceiling and floor joists above. Not nearly enough. Frustrated, Tori pulled the tile back into place and stepped off the toilet.

She might not be able to escape the room, but she could at least escape the hot confines of the caftan she wore. With a vicious yank she pulled it up and over her head, gritting her teeth as fabric tore away from the wounds on her wrists. Ripe with sweat and fear, the caftan wasn't worth returning. When the DEA released her, she'd send payment to Parinyah. *If* they released her.

"Tori?" Noah's voice sounded through the closed door, the deep rumble more welcome than it should have been.

She pulled open the door, stepping out into a room that teemed with people: Noah, Jack, Iceman, two men in suits and a woman who watched Tori with an expression bordering on distaste.

Tori straightened her spine, forcing energy into her posture and voice. "You're finally back. I was beginning to wonder if you planned to return."

"It took longer than expected to assemble and brief the team. We're here now, though. So why don't you have a seat and we'll get started." Jack gestured to the table and the three agents took seats.

Noah pulled out a chair and Tori sank into it. "I'd like to call my grandfather before we discuss things."

"There'll be plenty of time for that later." Jack's voice was too smooth, too calm.

"I thought I was going home later."

"You are." He didn't add *eventually,* though Tori was sure he was thinking it.

"Mr. McKenzie—"

"Call me Jack. I'll call you Tori. Makes things less formal that way." He sounded amiable enough, his light brown hair and hazel eyes too boy-next-door to seem dangerous, but Tori didn't miss the hard edge in his tone.

"Jack, then. I was told I'd be able to call my grandfather when I got here. I'd like to do that now."

"Twenty minutes. Then we'll break and you can make the call."

He took the seat closest to Tori, angling himself so he faced her, a look of patient understanding in his eyes. "So, tell me how you got the box."

"I bought it at a *wat* outside of Mae Hong Son."

"Wat Plam Neung?"

A purposeful mistake. No way had Jack forgotten what she'd told him on the phone. "Wat Doi Kong Mu."

"Right. And you went there because…"

"I was sightseeing."

"Kind of out of the way, isn't it? Especially for a lone woman." This from the female agent, her eyes black as coal and filled with malice.

"I wasn't alone. I went with a tour group."

"But still, you were alone with the group."

Tori gritted her teeth and nodded. "As alone as a person can be when she's with six or seven other people."

"You have the name of the tour guide?"

"No."

"Names of any of the people you were with?"

"No."

"So you arranged to go on a tour by yourself during a time that was supposed to be spent visiting a daughter you hadn't seen in five years?"

"Melody is the Raymonds' daughter."

"And yours. That's the reason you were in Thailand, right? To visit Melody."

"Yes, but the visit was over. I was leaving Mae Hong Son later that day."

"So you carried your packed bags on the tour?" A small-framed man spoke this time, his bright eyes boring into Tori's from behind thick-lensed glasses.

"I left them with friends of the Raymonds."

"And you remember their names? Or is that another bit of information you've forgotten?" The woman again, and this time Tori didn't bother hiding her irritation.

"Sorry to disappoint you, but I do remember. Chet and Parinyah Preteep. They own a jewelry shop in Mae Hong Son."

"No need to get upset, Tori. These are just routine questions." Jack smiled and tapped a pen against the table. "Why don't we backtrack a minute? Did you arrange to leave your bags with the Preteeps ahead of time?"

Tori forced back her temper and shook her head. "No. But I did arrange to meet with them. I had a locket I wanted copied as a gift for Melody. The Preteeps' jewelry designer was late and Chet suggested I take the tour while I waited. By the time I got back, the design had been drawn and an estimate was ready." And she had the box. The perfect container for a silver locket.

"Layne, check out the jeweler."

At Jack's words, the woman stood and left the room, one hard, dark look shot in Tori's direction before she moved out of sight.

"Tell us how you happened to buy the box." Jack leaned back in his chair, steepled his fingers under his chin and looked completely relaxed.

Tori was anything but. "Look, if you suspect me of something, why don't you just come out and say it?"

"*Suspect* is a strong word. *Curious* might be a better one." Another agent spoke this time. A bear of a man with hair tied back in a ponytail and a thick brown beard. "We've got certain connections. Sometimes we get lucky and are passed valuable information. This is one of those times. First we hear that the Wa are delivering key information to Lao and that Lao has arranged for an American to carry it to Bangkok. Then, less than a week later, we hear that Lao is holding an American woman. That she's got the information but refuses to give it up. Sounds to us like she got greedy. Maybe decided to take Lao for a little more than what they'd agreed on. And now, here you are, telling us it was all a mix-up, that you had no idea there was information on that box. Seems a little far-fetched."

"It can seem like whatever you want it to seem like, but the truth is I went into the souvenir shop to kill some time, saw a little rosewood box and thought Melody would like it. It had some scratches on the top, so I asked the store clerk if he had another like it. He went to look and came back with the box I bought."

"And after you bought it?" Jack leaned close, the pen tapping against the desk again.

Tori wanted to tear it from his hand and stomp it into the ground. "I gave the box to Chet. He agreed to put the locket in it and deliver both to Melody in a week."

"So he had the box when you left Mae Hong Son?"

"Yes."

"And you planned to return for it, when?"

"I already told you, I wasn't going to return for it. It was a gift for Melody."

"Sorry. I must have missed that. Tell me again why you decided to buy the box."

"Why don't you just lock me up now and get it over with?" She'd meant the words to be sarcastic. Instead they were weary.

"How about a cup of coffee, Red?" Noah's hand came to rest on her shoulder, its warmth seeping through her T-shirt and chasing away the chill she'd barely realized she was feeling. She wanted to lean in to his touch, borrow his strength, but doing so would only show how weak she really was.

"How about that phone call home?"

There was a moment of silence. Then Jack gave an almost imperceptible nod. "She can use the phone in my office."

Jack's office was two doors down from the room where Tori had been interrogated. She shifted her weight from foot to foot as she waited for Noah to give the operator the country code and phone number. When he held the phone out to her, she grabbed it, her hand shaking. It would be three in the afternoon at home. Pops might be at the diner getting a slice of pie, or visiting with his friends at the community center. Or he might be home, waiting for Tori's call.

The phone rang once. Then twice. She'd almost given up when the line clicked and a familiar voice filled the line. "Riley here."

"Pops..." She wanted to say more but the words caught in her throat.

"Tori? Where are you, girl? I've been out of my mind with worry."

"I'm still in Thailand."

"You were supposed to be home six days ago."

"I know. I ran into some trouble and—"

"Stay where you are. I'm coming to get you. We'll work the trouble out together."

"No!"

"What do you mean, 'No'? You think I'll sit over here in my easy chair while you get yourself out of whatever mess you're in? Ain't gonna happen. Got my passport yesterday. I'll be on the first plane I can get."

"I'm okay. Everything's okay. I just need another couple days, then I'll be home."

"A couple days are enough time for me to get there and make sure you make your flight."

And he would. She could see him now, striding from the plane, determined to take on the world. But he was aging despite his determination to stay active and strong. It would be so easy for someone to hurt him.

She gripped the cord tight, trying to make her voice sound reasonable and light. "Please don't come, Pops.

I'm okay. That's why I called. To let you know everything is fine."

"You've never been any good at lying."

"And you've always been good at seeing things that weren't there. I'm going to be okay, Pops. I promise."

"You'd better be. You're all I have left." His voice broke and Tori closed her eyes, trying to will away the image of Pops alone in his huge Victorian farmhouse, tears in his eyes.

"Can I speak to him?" Noah spoke close to her ear, the warmth of his breath against her neck sending a quiver along her spine.

Her eyes flew open, her back stiffening. "Pops, there's someone here who'd like to speak with you. He's—"

But the phone was already out of her hand, Noah standing in front of her, a slight smile easing the hard lines of his face. He mouthed a thank-you before speaking into the phone. "Mr. Riley? Noah Stone. Your granddaughter and I are at the DEA's office in Chiang Mai. We're doing everything we can to get her home as quickly as possible." He was silent for several long seconds, his blue-green eyes steady on Tori as he listened. "No. I agree. You've got every right to be worried, but by the time you get here, she could be on her way home. It'll do her more good to have you there waiting. Yes, I know, but she isn't alone. I'm here and I have every intention of getting her home. You can count on it. I look forward to meeting you, too." He handed the phone back to Tori.

"Pops?"

"That Noah Stone sounds like he's got his head on straight. You stay close to him, you hear me?"

"Yes."

"And when you get home I want the whole story."

"You'll get it."

"I've missed you, gal. You know that, don't you?"

"I know. I've missed you, too."

"Promise you'll be careful."

"Only if you promise to take your blood pressure medicine."

"You drive a hard bargain."

"Only because I love you."

"I love you, too. Now go get your troubles straightened out so you can come home."

"I will. Bye, Pops."

"Bye. Be good. Pray lots. I'll see you soon." The words were ones he'd spoken often when she was a teen, saying them each morning before she went to school. She'd forgotten the warmth and comfort she'd found in them.

"You're falling asleep on your feet." Noah slid an arm around her waist, and only then did Tori realize she'd closed her eyes again.

"Sorry. It's been a long few days." She forced her eyes open, tried to pull back, but Noah's grip didn't loosen, his fingers brushing against her side in a soft caress that sent heat to her cheeks. "We'd better get back. Jack must have a million more versions of the same question to ask."

"I'm going to tell Jack you've had enough for tonight."

"Think he'll listen?"

"He'll listen." Coming from anyone else, the statement might have sounded arrogant. Noah just sounded sure. As if he knew Jack well enough to predict what the man would or wouldn't do.

Or what he was thinking about Tori.

"Jack thinks I'm involved with Lao, doesn't he?"

"He's gathering the facts."

"I told him the facts. He doesn't believe me."

"His job isn't to believe or not. It's to find the truth."

"The truth is I haven't done anything wrong."

"I know."

"Do you?"

"Yeah. I do."

"Then tell Jack."

"I have."

"And?"

"And he has a job to do. He's doing it the best way he knows how." Noah tugged Tori out into the hall.

"I guess I've got to respect that. Even if it does land me in jail."

"You're not going to jail." Not if Noah had anything to do with it.

Tori nodded, but her dark eyes said she didn't believe him.

There wasn't time to reassure her. The door to the interrogation room swung open and Jack stepped into the hall, Jones, Mulligan and Valentine right behind him. On the surface they looked relaxed, but tension hung in the air around them, and Noah knew he wasn't going to like what they had to say.

Jack flashed his best "I'm on your side" smile and spoke into the heavy silence. "We were just coming to find you. It's late. We're all tired. I think it's time to call it a night."

An hour ago Jack had been determined to question Tori until he got the answers he wanted. Now he'd decided she'd had enough for the night. Noah didn't ask what had happened to change his mind. Not yet. He'd wait until Tori was settled. "I was going to suggest the same thing."

"We've got a room upstairs for you, Tori. Nothing fancy, just a futon and a bathroom with a shower, but you won't be there long, anyway." Jack put his hand under Tori's elbow, and Noah was sure her muscles tensed.

Apparently she wasn't buying the act, either.

Like Noah, she kept her thoughts to herself, allowing Jack to lead her onto the elevator. Noah stepped on behind them, shooting the rest of the team a warning look. "We'll meet you back down here after Tori gets settled in."

Valentine opened her mouth to argue, but Jack cut her off. "We'll see you in a few."

The door slid shut and the elevator jerked to life.

Tori wasn't sure what was going on, but she knew it wasn't good. She didn't bother asking. What would be the point? Jack would tell her what he wanted to, and Tori wasn't convinced that would be the truth.

"Here we are." The room looked like an office, a desk against one wall, a file cabinet next to it. Both were dull gray and well-worn. No windows, no phone, just plain white walls and a wood door that must lead to the bathroom. Only the futon looked comfortable, the deep blue fabric so crisp Tori felt sure it was new.

"You'll be comfortable here for now. Shower's through that door. I had Layne buy a few things. Soap, shampoo and clothes. She guessed on the size, so let's hope they work." Jack's smile didn't reach his eyes.

"I appreciate it."

"I'll have someone bring up some food."

"I'm—"

"Food'll do you good, Red."

She didn't have the energy to argue. "Right. Thanks."

"We'll be downstairs. You need anything, press one on this." Jack handed her what looked like a very small cell phone.

"A phone?"

"More like a pager."

"Guess I won't be calling any friends, then."

Noah ignored her poor attempt at humor. "You'll be getting the sleep you obviously need. Here, Joi gave me a few things she thought you might want." He took off his pack and pulled out a bundle of cloth.

"Thank you."

"No problem. Now stop worrying. Get some sleep. We'll talk more later."

He and Jack walked out of the room, the soft thud of the door and gentle click of a lock being turned echoing loudly in the silent room.

Chapter Eight

The bathroom was sparse. White toilet, white sink and a tiny tiled shower. A window set high on the wall and covered in dull black paint let in none of the outside world.

"Definitely a prison." Tori muttered the words as she pulled jeans and a T-shirt from the bundle Joi had sent. A small leather Bible fell on the floor near her feet and she picked it up, shoving it onto the ledge of the sink.

The shower ran cold, then lukewarm, and Tori was in and out quickly. Dressed in the jeans and T-shirt, she tried to work her fingers through tangled curls, but gave up when her wrists began to bleed again, the blood trickling down her forearms, trailing pink rivulets into the sink. She pressed a towel against the wounds, then grabbed the Bible and stepped from the bathroom, eyeing the small leather book and wishing she could find comfort in its pages. But God's promises were for those with faith, and her faith had died long ago.

She sighed, set the Bible down on the futon, the need to move clawing at her gut. Where were Noah and Jack? What secrets were they hiding from her?

She twisted the doorknob, was surprised when it turned beneath her hand and the door swung open. She took the elevator down, stepped out and walked into Noah's broad, firm chest.

His hand came around her forearms, holding her in place when she might have fallen backward. "Aren't you supposed to be sleeping?"

"Not until I find out what's going on."

His jaw tightened, his eyes stormy. "Melody's missing."

The ground shifted beneath her feet, blackness threatening. "When? How?"

"Maybe a couple of hours. Joi couldn't sleep and went to check on her. Melody's bed was empty. I was just coming up to tell you."

"No." It was all she could force out.

"Hawke's got men out searching. The Royal Thai Police are putting together a search party. I'm heading back to Mae Hong Son to join them."

"Let's go."

"I'm going alone."

"And I'm supposed to sit here twiddling my thumbs? I don't think so." She was already turning back toward the elevator, intent on getting upstairs, grabbing the money she'd shoved in her pants pocket earlier in the day. It would be enough to get her back to Mae Hong Son.

Noah pulled her back, his eyes flashing fire, his jaw granite hard. "You don't have a choice."

"Sure I do. I can walk out of here and find my own way to Mae Hong Son."

"Too dangerous." Jack spoke from behind Tori, his words quiet but filled with authority.

She turned to face him, anger and fear making her reckless. "If I want to leave, I'll leave."

"And do what? Do you think you'll be helping Melody by handing yourself over to Lao? Once he has you, he'll demand you return the box. You tell him the DEA's got it and neither you nor Melody will survive."

"So give me the box. Let me return it to them."

"It doesn't work that way. *We* don't work that way." The words were hard, but it was the pity in his eyes that had Tori turning away and slamming her hand against the elevator call button.

When the doors didn't open right away, she slammed her fist against the button again and again, not feeling the pain of impact—feeling nothing but the terror of her own impotence.

"Enough." Noah's hand wrapped around hers, forcing it down.

She spun toward him, fury a hot knot in her stomach. "You said Melody would be safe. You told me Hawke would make sure nothing happened."

"I know. I'm sorry."

"*Sorry?* Is that supposed to help?" Her voice shook, her body vibrating with rage and with fear.

Jack pushed himself between Tori and Noah, his lips tight with anger. "No one could have predicted this."

"And that makes it all right? Melody's thirteen. A baby." The elevator doors slid open and she turned, stumbling through them, willing them to shut before either man spoke again, before the tears she was holding back escaped.

But Jack wasn't willing to let things go. He stood in the door, his eyes so hard and cold, Tori shrank against the wall of the elevator.

"Listen to me, Tori. Nothing that's happened here is Noah's fault. Nor is it the fault of the DEA. We took every precaution, did everything we could to make sure Melody was safe. But Lao's after what you took from him. He won't stop until he gets it. Maybe you should have thought of that before you crossed him."

"I didn't—"

But Jack had already stepped off the elevator. The doors slid shut, closing Tori in with her fear and with her guilt.

"You think that was necessary?" Noah eyed the man who'd once been his boss, fighting the urge to shove past him, slam his hand against the button and call the elevator back down.

Jack shrugged, the coldness he'd shown Tori gone. "I want the truth. Whatever that might be. And I'll do what I have to to get it."

"You've gotten everything you will from her."

"Maybe."

"She's innocent. Eventually your investigation will prove it."

"Until then I'll keep pushing."

"Don't push too hard. She's been through a lot."

"She's getting to you, isn't she?"

"The case is getting to me. Having a thirteen-year-old kid taken from the safe house I arranged is getting to me."

"You did your best to keep Melody and her family safe."

"Then my best wasn't good enough."

"We can't save everyone every time. I wish we could, but we can't. This might be one of those times—"

"Not this time. Not this kid." Noah shoved open the door to Jack's office and stalked across the room, his mind filled with images of another place, another child. One he hadn't saved.

"Even if you save her, it won't change what happened two years ago."

"Won't change it, but at least I won't have more nightmares to add to the ones already keeping me awake at night."

"More guilt, you mean. When are you going to let it go, Noah? What happened wasn't your fault, and if the Raymond girl doesn't survive, that won't be your fault, either."

"It'll feel like it is." He grabbed his pack from Jack's desk. "Chase is on his way?"

Jack looked like he wanted to say more about guilt and about the past, but he knew Noah well enough not to push the issue. "Said he'll be ready to lift off in half an hour."

"Good. The sooner we hit Mae Hong Son, the better I'll feel."

"Me, too." Jack paused, watched as Noah checked his gun and holstered it in the shoulder strap he wore under his T-shirt. "You never answered my question."

Noah tensed. "Which one?"

"The one about Tori Riley. Is she getting to you? Should I put someone else on this case?"

"She's not getting to me."

He didn't look like he believed Noah, but didn't push for more. "Good."

"I'll check in when I get to Mae Hong Son. We'll—" A loud buzz interrupted his words, and Noah waited while Jack lifted the phone.

"Yeah? No. Let her go. We'll get her when she hits the lobby." He hung up, sighed. "Looks like Tori doesn't plan to stay put."

"Where is she?"

"The stairwell."

"You've got a guard there?"

"We rigged the door on her floor with an alarm. Just in case. Not that she's got anywhere to go from there. The lobby is guarded."

And knowing Tori she'd already thought that through. So where did she think she was heading?

The roof.

It was the obvious escape route. Though not the safest. Would she chance it? He didn't know, but he planned to find out. "I'm out of here."

"Keep me updated."

"I will." Noah shrugged on his pack, wincing as stiff muscles in his shoulder tightened. On the heels of all that had happened, the reminder of the Wa's brutality wasn't welcome. But God was greater than the enemy, and Noah would have to trust Him to keep Melody safe. Just as he trusted God to help him make the right decision if he walked outside and found Tori making the leap from one building to the next, hoping to escape by way of the offices next door.

"Watch your back out there. I've got men flying in from Bangkok, but it'll take a few hours for them to make Mae Hong Son." Jack followed Noah as he stepped into the hall and headed for the door.

"The fewer agents we've got wandering around out there, the better. Sang Lao's desperate. We spook him, and he might kill the girl."

"He's got nothing without the girl, and he's smart

enough to know it, but don't worry—everyone's been briefed. Lao won't even know they're there. Now get moving. The girl's time is running out."

Tori stood on the roof and eyed the building next door. Five feet away. Not much more than one giant step. She'd jumped streams that were wider. But five feet might as well be the Grand Canyon when there were three stories of emptiness below. She took a step closer to the edge, stared down into a dimly lit alley. Her heart thundered with the weight of what she was about to do—leap across the chasm, find a way into the building next door. *Run from the DEA.*

If Jack hadn't thought she was guilty before, he would now.

But how could she do anything else? Melody was out there somewhere. Alone. Scared. Just as Tori had been so many years ago.

Please, let me find her. Please let her be okay.

As prayers went, it seemed useless, spiraling up into the night sky, bouncing into the darkness, fruitless and empty. But it was the best she could do, the most she could hope for.

She took several stiff-legged steps back, inhaled deeply and raced toward the edge of the roof. The world fell away, cement gone, nothing beneath her feet but air. Tori leaned forward, a scream she didn't dare release filling her head as she landed with a thud, momentum carrying her a few feet farther before she could stop herself. "Thank You, God. Thank You, God. Thank You, God."

She was still chanting the words as she tried the door that led into the building. Locked. She twisted the handle again with the same result. Okay. There had to be another way down. She just needed to find it.

Tori moved across the roof, cautious, quiet, ears straining for sounds of pursuit, eyes scanning the area, searching for something she wasn't sure she would find.

And if she didn't?

What then? Jump back across the chasm, go to her room and wait for news? Doing so would drive her mad with fear and worry. She'd be better off waiting on the roof until dawn. Maybe someone would arrive and open the door to the building. Of course, by that point Jack would have realized she was missing and sent men out looking for her.

She was about to try the door again when she saw it. At the far edge of the roof, a ladder of some sort. She hurried forward, saw the rusted edges of what could only be a fire escape. Though to Tori it looked more like a recipe for disaster. She shook the metal, tried to shove it away from the wall. When it held firm, she lowered herself over the side of the building, found her footing and started down.

One rung. Two. Five. She was starting to think she'd make it to the ground without killing herself when her questing foot met empty air. She stretched her leg down, searching for another rung and found nothing.

Now she had two choices—go back up or lower herself as far down as she could before dropping to the ground. The first would get her nowhere. The second might get her a broken ankle. She clutched the ladder with both hands, leaning her forehead against the building as she tried to decide what to do.

The scuff of footsteps against pavement drifted on the quiet air, and Tori froze, holding her breath, praying whoever was coming would pass by without seeing her.

Chapter Nine

"Need a hand?" Noah's voice was such a shock, Tori almost released her grip on the ladder.

A glance down into the alley revealed his shadowy figure in the darkness, just below her perch. "You scared me, again."

"And you scared me. That leap between the buildings cost me three years of my life."

"You didn't have to watch."

"I couldn't look away. Come on. Let's get you down from there before the ladder gives and your death-defying leap goes to waste."

"I guess you have a suggestion?"

"Sure do. Jump."

"It's twelve feet down!"

"More like twenty, but all you have to do is hang from the last rung and drop. I'll catch you."

She wanted to do what he suggested, but her hands stayed glued to the rung, every muscle in her body screaming that letting go was the last thing she should do.

"Come on, Red, you can do this. Lower yourself down and let go. It'll be a piece of cake."

"I don't like cake."

"Pie?"

"Only if it's apple."

"With ice cream?"

"Is there any other way to eat it?" She spoke as she adjusted her weight, pushing her feet against the wall beneath the last rung as she maneuvered down the rest of the ladder.

"At last, we agree on something." His voice was light, but Tori could sense his tension. He might be trying to keep her mind off how far up she was, but he wasn't nearly as relaxed about it as he was acting.

"Feet off the wall. Let yourself hang."

She gritted her teeth, commanded her body to cooperate, and let her legs fall out from under her, the pain in her wrists and side stealing her breath.

"You okay?"

"Yes. Fine. Tell me when you're ready. I don't want to hurt you when I drop."

Noah almost laughed at that. Despite her height, Tori had a fragile build. Catching her would be easy. It was convincing her to let go he was worried about. "Ready."

"Maybe I should go back up."

"Not your style."

"I wish I were as confident of that as you are. Brace yourself. Here I come."

To her credit she didn't make a sound as she dropped. No scream, no gasp, not even a whimper. He caught her easily, his hands grasping her waist as he eased her down to the ground.

"There you go. Safe on solid ground."

"Thanks for the help." She took a step away, and Noah snagged the back of her T-shirt, the heavy weight of her hair falling against his hand, damp and redolent with flowery shampoo. Her normal choice? Or would she go for something less feminine, more unique?

He pushed the questions aside, uncomfortable with the direction his thoughts were taking. "Mind if I ask where you're going?"

"The same place you're going. To find Melody."

"And you thought you could do that on your own?"

"I won't need to *do* anything."

She didn't expand on her plan. She didn't need to. Noah knew exactly what she was thinking, could even understand why. "So you'll let Lao's men find you. Let them bring you to Melody."

"Whatever works."

"Even if it means you and Melody both die?"

"It won't. Not if I have anything to do with it."

"When Sang Lao finds out you don't have the box, he'll have no use for you."

"I'll tell him the box is hidden. Buy some time."

"You're in over your head. This isn't a game for amateurs. Sang Lao is a cold-blooded killer and he's desperate. Think of what you went through when his men had you. Do you want that for Melody?"

"You know I don't." Her voice was hoarse, her words harsh, but at least he was getting through to her.

"Then go back to Jack. Stay there."

"And wait for Lao to find out I'm cooperating with the DEA? You know he will. The guard at the airport will talk. Or someone who saw me get off the helicopter in Chiang Mai will tell a friend who'll tell a friend.

One way or another, Lao will find out and when he does, Melody's dead."

"And wandering around by yourself will solve that problem?"

"It will buy us some time. That's all I'm worried about right now."

"It will put you right back into the midst of danger. Right back in the kind of situation I just got you out of."

"So? Do you think that matters to me? What matters is getting Melody away from Lao."

"At the risk of your safety."

"You don't seem to understand that my safety isn't what's important."

The problem was he did understand. He knew exactly what it felt like to have someone's life hang in the balance and to know that whatever decision was made would mean the difference between life and death. "You're wrong. I do understand."

"Then don't ask me to go back." Her face was a pale oval in the darkness, her eyes beseeching.

Despite the tremor in her voice, despite her apparent willingness to accede to his wishes, Noah knew that if he brought Tori back to Jack, she'd search for another means of escape. And next time he wouldn't be around to make sure she didn't succeed, or that she wasn't hurt in the attempt.

"Come on, let's go." He grabbed her hand, not releasing his grip as she tugged against his hold.

"I told you, I'm not going back."

"Who said I was bringing you back?"

"You're not?"

"Not if you agree to do exactly what I say, when I

say it, no arguments. You try going your own way and you'll be back here so fast your head'll spin."

She hesitated, then nodded. "Okay."

"Then let's go. Chase is waiting."

Her hand relaxed, her fingers twining with his, holding on in an unconscious gesture of trust that speared Noah's heart and made him all the more determined to make sure Tori and Melody made it through this experience unscathed.

The helicopter ride back to Mae Hong Son was made in silence. That suited Tori. Her mind was too filled with worry and fear to allow for idle chatter. Noah's words echoed through her mind, his reminder of what she'd suffered, what Melody might already be suffering, a physical blow that left her shaken. Had giving her daughter up been for nothing? Had the decision she'd made thirteen years ago led to this—Melody's kidnapping, her torture, maybe even her death?

Tori wouldn't believe that. She couldn't. The Raymonds deserved more than that. Melody deserved more.

But life wasn't about getting what one deserved. Hadn't Tori's childhood proven that? She shuddered, her mind flashing back to times better forgotten. Harsh words, the sting of a hand against her cheek, locked doors, locked hearts, the futile attempt to be loved for who and what she was.

"We're here." The tinny sound of Chase's voice drew Tori away from the past. Which was good. Dwelling on things that couldn't be changed never accomplished anything.

Below, the helicopter pad was a bright light in an otherwise dark landscape. Soon they'd be back at the safe house. Maybe they'd find answers there. Tori wasn't counting on it. She doubted Noah was, either. Her gaze strayed to his profile. Strong, determined and capable. All the things Tori once thought she wanted in a man. Of course, that had been when she'd actually considered marriage as an option in her life. Two broken engagements later, she knew better. She had a knack for picking men who were surface-perfect and seriously flawed inside.

"Let's go." Noah helped Tori off the helicopter, his hand firm on her elbow as she stepped out in the rushing rotor-wind. They waited near the airport door as the helicopter lifted off and the air settled to stillness around them. "Simon should be waiting out front. He'll take us to the safe house."

"And once we get there?"

"Gather the facts. Find out what areas the search parties are covering. Pray someone, somewhere, knows something and is willing to share the information."

"And if no one does?"

"Then we'll keep looking." The answer was short, almost abrupt, as if Noah didn't want to waste time or energy explaining things.

Tori didn't blame him for that. Things had gone from bad to worse in the past few hours, and her decision to leave the DEA's headquarters had only added to whatever burden Noah felt. "I'm sorry about all this."

He glanced her way as they moved around the corner of the building, hugging the wall and staying in deep shadows. "About what?"

"Putting you in this position. Forcing you to bring me here."

"I don't ever get forced into something I don't want to do."

"Yet you're here."

"Not by force."

"You're retired. There must have been a reason for that."

"I was injured. Had to take a step back and reassess my life. That doesn't mean I can't take a job when asked. Stop." He pressed her back into the shadows and let out the same high-pitched whistle he'd used earlier.

Simon's answer cut through the early-morning stillness and Noah put his hand on Tori's lower back, guiding her out into the open. Shadows danced at the perimeter of the parking lot, and she imagined eyes staring at her from their depths. Her heart thrummed a quick, nervous beat, her terror morphing into a steady hum of panic.

"Hopefully, your injury didn't affect your gun arm. You'll probably need to use it before this is over." The comment was flip, foolish, and Tori regretted it as soon as it was out. "Sorry. I talk too much when I'm nervous."

"Two years of physical therapy's fixed what's broken. I'm not active DEA because I choose not to be. Not because I can't be." The words were dry, Noah's gaze still scanning the perimeter of the parking lot as he led Tori to Simon's car.

He pulled open the back door, and Tori got in, her stomach aching with guilt. Noah had put his life on the line to save hers and she'd repaid him by making a callous remark about an injury that had obviously been very serious. "Noah—"

He turned to face her. "Let it go. I'm not upset and you shouldn't be, either."

Before she could say anything else, Simon started the engine and Noah turned his attention to the other man, all the kind reassurance in his voice gone. "Any news?"

"We found the traitor." Simon spit the words out, his anger obvious.

"Who is he?"

"She. Woman's been working for my brother for five years. Seemed loyal. Until tonight."

"What's she saying?"

"Nothing. She's dead. Found her body in the jungle behind the compound. Near as we can figure, she put out the call as soon as the Raymonds arrived. Made contact with someone in Lao's organization."

"Any idea how she got the girl out?"

"Drugged her partner. They were on security duty, manning the cameras. Once he was out of it, she turned off the alarm system, drugged the girl and carried her out of the house. We found a hypodermic needle on the floor beside the girl's bed."

Tori closed her eyes, refusing to think of the terror Melody must have felt when she'd woken up to the pain of a needle stabbing into her flesh.

"There was a note pinned to the woman's body." Simon continued, his voice cold and hard as steel.

"Lao's demands?"

"He wants Tori and the box within twenty-four hours. Not a lot of time."

"We'll make it work." Noah sounded confident, but Tori wondered what he really thought—if he actually believed they'd find Melody before then.

"You know how many acres of land we've got to cover?" Simon's question voiced the doubts Tori felt.

"About as well as anyone."

"Then you know searching for the girl will be like searching a ten-story haystack for a crumb of bread."

"Not quite as bad as that. I've got contacts. So do you and Hawke. We've got the manpower. It's just a matter of time before we get a lead."

"Time that we don't have. Like I said, there's not a chance in—"

"Watch it, we've got a lady present."

Simon grunted, stepping on the accelerator and speeding up a steep incline. Sparse buildings gave way to thick jungle, the lights of Mae Hong Son disappearing behind the car. It didn't take long to reach the safe house. Illuminated by spotlights, the yard filled with men and women, it looked nothing like the silent, brooding house of hours ago.

Hawke stood on the front stoop, his scar a dark slash across his cheek. When the car pulled to a stop, he moved toward it, his steps strong and purposeful, energy and anger seeping off him in waves. He yanked Tori's door open, but didn't acknowledge her in any way, just stepped back and waited for Noah to climb from the car. "I thought maybe you weren't going to make the party."

"I got detained on the way to the airport."

"I can see that." Pale gray eyes raked over Tori. "She staying here?"

"Coming with me."

"Probably better that way. Coffee's inside. Better get some now. We head out in an hour."

"I'll meet you out here in ten minutes. We'll go over the plans. Ready, Tori?" He put his hand on her elbow and started moving her toward the house.

She held back, not wanting to waste a minute of the

time they had. "I don't want coffee, and we don't have an hour to spare."

"We've got an hour whether we can spare it or not. Why not spend the time with the Raymonds?" He let his hand drop from her arm, smoothed it along the contour of her back, the gesture comforting and all too welcome.

She wanted to lean her head against his shoulder, let him take control. But doing so could only lead to disappointment. She straightened her spine, tried to ignore the warmth of his fingers against her neck, the gentle kneading of his hand against tense muscles there. "The Raymonds want their daughter found. They'll understand if I don't take the time to stop and chat. We need to be out searching, not standing around doing nothing."

"Setting up a search and rescue takes time. Rushing out without being prepared is the worst thing any of us can do."

She knew he was right, knew that rushing out without a plan would be of no benefit to Melody. That didn't mean she liked it. Or that she was ready to face the Raymonds. "How can I face Joi and Mark when their daughter is missing because of me?"

She hadn't meant to say the words out loud, and stepped away from Noah, not wanting to see the pity in his eyes.

"How can you not when you know how much you mean to them?" The words were quiet, the fingers that brushed her cheek so gentle she barely felt their featherlight touch as Noah hooked a strand of hair behind her ear.

"I—"

His hand dropped to her jaw, urged her to look up, meet his gaze. "You're no coward, Red. Go in. Let them see you're okay. Give them at least that small comfort."

Not a coward? He had a lot more faith in her than she had in herself. And that was something she hadn't expected, didn't want, but knew she couldn't ignore.

Tori swallowed back the lump in her throat. "Okay. Let's go."

He smiled, drew her close in a hug that threatened to destroy all her defenses.

Shaken, she pulled back, hurrying into the house and away from Noah.

Hadn't she learned her lesson the hard way? Hadn't she found out that depending on others, trusting them, only led to disappointment? Noah might seem like a good guy with strong convictions, but Tori had known plenty of people who seemed to be one thing and were something quite different. When she'd found Kyle going through her grandfather's paperwork, she'd vowed that she'd never be vulnerable again, that she'd never again let herself be duped by surface kindness and fake integrity. She had no intention of breaking that promise.

And that meant keeping her distance from Noah. Not letting him get past the defenses she'd worked so hard to erect. But even as she told herself that she could do it, that keeping Noah at arm's length would be easy, she couldn't help wondering if it was already too late. If Noah had already done what she hadn't allowed anyone to do in years—touch her heart.

Chapter Ten

Noah followed Tori into the house, wondering at her reaction and at the moisture he'd seen in her eyes. How much longer could she keep going? How much further could she push herself? He didn't know and wasn't sure finding out was an option. Staying here with the Raymonds might be best for everyone concerned, though the thought of leaving her, of giving her the opportunity to take off on her own made his skin crawl and his gut clench.

Joi and Mark were in the living room, huddled together on the couch, hands clasped, heads bent—praying, Noah knew, for the daughter who'd been taken from them. Tori stood on the threshold, her silence and stillness saying she respected their faith, even if she didn't believe in it.

Joi must have sensed her presence. She glanced up, her face smudged with moisture as she leapt to her feet. "Tori." That was all she managed before tears choked off her words and slid down her cheeks.

"Oh, Joi, I'm so sorry." Tori's voice broke, and she wrapped Joi in her arms.

"We'll get her back." Mark stood and patted Tori's shoulder, his other hand pressed to his wife's back. Together the three seemed to close ranks against the world, their private agony something that couldn't be shared.

Noah shifted from foot to foot, his own throat tight as he witnessed something he'd hoped never to see again—the anguish of a family torn apart.

Images flashed through his mind, painted in excruciating detail. Dark blue silk, black hair, a red river of blood flowing from beneath a small, broken body. Sing Lee kneeling on the ground, the child held in her hands, her eyes wild with grief. Her husband lying still as death just yards away. All of it washed in the shadowy gray of pain.

As if she could sense the horror of what Noah had lived, Tori's head jerked up, her eyes dark, her brow furrowed. "Noah?"

She didn't ask if he was okay, but the question was there in her eyes, in the way she tensed and pulled back from Joi just a little.

"I'm going to get coffee." He turned and strode into the kitchen, grabbing the coffeepot, pouring scorching liquid into a heavy ceramic mug, drinking it fast, the bitter fire of it burning a trail down his throat. But nothing could burn away the memories.

"You won't be able to taste food for a week." Tori hovered in the doorway, her eyes filled with worry.

He shrugged and put the mug on the counter. "How are the Raymonds doing?"

"About as well as can be expected. Which isn't all that good."

"They're strong people. They'll be okay."

"I know, but it still hurts to see them like this. It

hurts even more to know that Melody's twice as scared. Maybe hurt. Maybe worse."

"She's Lao's key to you and the box. He won't harm her until he has both in his grasp."

She shrugged, moving past him, the flowery scent he'd noticed before drifting on the air as she grabbed a mug from a hook above the sink and poured coffee. "I wish I had your faith. Right now things seem so futile."

"Nothing is futile, Red."

"You really believe that?" She eyed him over the rim of the cup, the dark crescents under her eyes stark against the white of her skin.

"Yeah. I do. Come here." He took the cup from her hand, put it on the counter and pulled her into his arms. He wasn't sure what he'd expected, only knew he was surprised when her head fell forward against his chest, flame-red hair hiding her face.

She sniffed, shuddered, her muscles tense with the emotions she held in check.

"It's okay to cry, you know."

"No, it isn't, because if I start I might never stop." Her hands slid around his waist, holding tight for mere seconds before she released her grip and pulled away. "We should bring the Raymonds some coffee."

The change in subject was obvious, her intent clear—push aside her feelings, deal with the mundane. Who was he to force her to do anything else? "How about juice? They might be too jumpy for coffee."

"How about both? Then they can choose themselves."

"There you go, a compromise. I always knew we'd get along."

"You did not. You thought I was a drug trafficker."

"I had serious doubts about that." He opened cupboards, found two glasses.

"Did you? Why?"

"Your eyes. They tell the truth, even when you don't."

She shrugged, turning to face him, a cup of coffee in each hand, her cheeks tinged pink. "Guess that explains why my grandparents always knew when I was lying."

"You lied often?"

"No, but I tried. Luckily, Pops and Gran were very firm and very forgiving." She strode past him, her quick exit cutting off any comments Noah might have made.

Joi and Mark sat side by side on the couch, arms wrapped around each other, heads bent close together once again. They looked up as Tori entered the room, but this time neither rose, as if the past few hours had drained them of all energy.

"We've got coffee and juice."

"Thanks." Mark reached for the coffee, took a sip. "Hawke's looking for you, Noah."

"Thanks. I'll be back in a few minutes. By then it should almost be time to head out."

"You're not planning to sneak off without me?" The tone was light, but Tori's eyes begged for reassurance.

"No, I'll come back for you. Just make sure you don't get restless and come looking." He stepped out into the hall and disappeared from sight.

As soon as he was gone, Joi stood and put a hand on Tori's arm. "Is it a good idea for you to go with him? You're battered and exhausted. Searching through the jungle will only make things worse."

"I'd rather be out searching than in here waiting."

"You never could stand to wait for anything." Mark

rubbed a hand along the back of his neck and watched Tori through deeply shadowed eyes.

"Remember the week before Melody was born? You wore a hole in the floor with all your pacing." Joi smiled at the memory, not trying to hide the tears that slid down her cheeks.

Tori's own tears burned hot and insistent behind her eyes. "I remember. I thought she'd never come, and then once she did, I wanted so badly to have that time with her again." The words slipped out, and Tori turned away, ready to rush from the room.

But Noah was there, back much sooner than he should have been, blocking the path to the door.

If there'd been pity in his eyes she might have shoved past. Instead, she saw understanding and something else. Something she refused to put a name to. She looked at the door behind him, the floor, anything but his eyes. "Did you find Hawke?"

"Yeah. Mark, he'd like to speak to you, as well."

Mark stood, the lines on his face obvious in the harsh overhead light. "Good. Sitting here was making me antsy."

"I'll come with you." But before Tori could move through the doorway, Noah put a hand out to stop her.

"We'll be leaving soon. The best thing you can do right now is have something to drink. Maybe grab a piece of fruit from the kitchen. You're going to need strength to get through the next few hours."

He didn't give her a chance to argue, just stepped away and strode down the hall, Mark close on his heels.

Tori took a step after them, but Joi's voice stopped her. "Don't bother. They'll just escort you back in."

"It's like some macho, male-only club. They head

out into danger, and we stay safely tucked away inside." Tori slumped down onto the couch, ignoring the pain that danced through her rib cage as she did so.

"They mean well. They're just worried. Melody's already been taken. What's to keep us from being next?"

"I know. I just wish..."

"Wish what?"

"That I'd stayed in Lakeview. If I had, none of this would have happened."

Joi shook her head, a smile easing the lines of worry around her eyes and mouth. "You've always been so sure that every bad thing that happens is because of something you've done."

"And this time I'm right. The fact is, if I'd stayed home, you'd all be safe at the clinic right now."

"I think you're taking too much responsibility for this. Sometimes things just happen. Bad things. Good things. Not because of what we've done or not done. Just because the world is a fallen, sinful place."

Tori wasn't sure she agreed, but she didn't argue. What would be the point? Fault or no, Melody had been taken. She was alone somewhere, scared, unsure. Maybe hurt. Tori pinched the bridge of her nose, trying to force back hot tears.

"Tori." Joi put a hand against Tori's cheek, the gesture so sweet, so much like what a mother might do to comfort her child, that one of the tears Tori was holding back escaped. She blinked back more, moving away, standing up, knowing that if her own mother had ever once done the same, she might have believed there was hope for having a relationship with her.

Joi followed Tori up, reaching out again, this time putting her hand on Tori's arm, holding tight, as if she could will her faith into Tori's doubting spirit. "Melody is going to be okay. We have to believe that. We have to have faith that God will protect her."

Tori wasn't even sure she knew what faith was, but she smiled anyway, forcing her own doubts aside for the sake of her friend. "Of course He will."

"And Melody's a fighter, just like you. She may already have escaped."

Again, Tori kept her own counsel, not willing to tell Joi that escaping Lao had proven impossible for her and that, without Noah's intervention, she might still be chained to a wall in Chiang Mai. "Melody *is* a fighter, but I'd say she gets that from you and Mark. You two have never been afraid of anything."

"Does it seem that way? I've been afraid of plenty in my life. Afraid of never being a mother, afraid of not being a good enough mother, afraid of coming to Thailand, afraid of not coming to Thailand." Joi stepped across the room and stared out the window. "Do you remember the day we met?"

"Vividly. I'd dyed my hair blue the night before, put on black lipstick. I figured there was no way Pops and Gran would bring me to church looking like that."

"You were so wrong." Joi's laughter was soft and a little sad. "I think your grandfather had you by the ear and was tugging you into the back pew when Eliza Jean nudged me in the ribs and said, 'Look what Sam and Anna just dragged into church.' I looked up from my choir book, saw you and I knew we were going to be friends."

"What clued you in? The blue hair, the black lipstick or my scowl?"

"Your eyes. They were saying the same thing mine

always seemed to say when I looked in the mirror—that you were alone, and sad, and wished there was just one person in the world that understood."

"I never knew you felt that way, Joi."

"No one did. Not even Mark. My life was so easy, so blessed—how could I complain?" She turned to face Tori. "But my arms were empty, and there were days that was all I could think about. Then you came along and suddenly there was more to my life than my husband, my job, church, my empty womb. You changed my life for the better before you ever told me you were pregnant and offered me your child. Whatever happens, I'll always feel that way."

"Joi—"

Before Tori could decide what she wanted to say, Noah and Mark stepped back into the room.

Mark hurried to his wife, threw an arm around her shoulders and pulled her close. "We've got news. Do you remember Samrarn Tinawong?"

Joi started to shake her head, then paused. "Wait. Wasn't he a tribal leader? Blue H'mong? Came to the clinic a few months ago. His son had been bitten by a king cobra."

"That's right. We started the antivenom and had Prawit Medevacked to the hospital in Chiang Mai."

"He survived, didn't he?"

"By the grace of God. I haven't seen many people that close to death pull through." Mark paced across the room, as if he couldn't stay still. "Samrarn told us we'd always be family after that. Remember?"

"Yes, but what—"

"He heard some commotion in the jungle a couple of hours ago and sent some men out to investigate."

"Commotion?" Tori's mind raced with the possibility of what that could mean.

"Voices. Branches breaking. Not something he'd usually hear at one or two in the morning." As he spoke, Noah spread a map across the back of the couch and traced his finger along an imaginary line. "He was worried about thieves. The village has had some livestock stolen recently. Instead of thieves, his men spotted a troop of heavily armed soldiers."

"Was Melody with them?" Joi stepped forward, hope lighting her face.

"We don't know. Samrarn's men didn't dare get too close. They did hear talk of Hawke and the missionary girl who'd been taken from his compound. Melody's name was mentioned, but not whether she was with them or where they were headed. Samrarn's had dealings with Hawke before and decided to send a message here with the information."

"So now we have a starting point." The thought filled Tori with more hope than she'd had in hours.

"Exactly. We'll head here first," Noah pointed to a spot on the map. "Talk to Samrarn, see if he has any more information. Then we'll search all the villages within walking distance of his."

"How many is that?"

"Quite a few. But only three or four that are known to affiliate with Lao and the Wa."

"When do we leave?"

"Now."

"I'd like to come, too." Mark stepped forward.

"Mark, no!" Joi's words were a horrified cry.

"Honey, I—"

Noah didn't let him finish. He just put a hand on his

shoulder and spoke in a quiet, calm voice. "If Melody were my daughter, I'd feel the same. But the best thing you can do for her is be here when she gets back. She'll need you, healthy and alive. You go out on the search, there's a good possibility that won't be what she gets. Remember, the men and women who are part of the search team are trained in search and rescue. They know the area. They're prepared."

"Tori isn't. Wouldn't it be better for her to stay, too?" Mark's voice was filled with frustration.

"Tori sticks with me." Noah left it at that, not even hinting at the truth—that the DEA suspected she was involved with Lao, that she was not just a witness but a suspect, and that Jack had threatened Noah with jail time if Tori managed to escape from him.

Mark didn't look happy, but nodded his head. "Guess we're wasting time discussing it. Let's pray and get the two of you out of here."

Ten minutes later, Tori stood in the yard with scores of other men and women. Some wore the khaki uniform of the Royal Thai Police. Others were in military uniform. Still others were civilians. Or dressed as such. The group was large, the hushed conversation a quiet hum in the stillness of early morning. Already, the first rays of gold and pink stretched across the sky, touching the mountains and deep green jungle. Soon it would be full daylight.

Time was passing too quickly.

Tori shivered, rubbing her arms against a nonexistent chill.

"You cold?" Noah spoke close to her ear, his dark hair whispering against her cheek.

"Scared." The truth slipped out, and she bit her lip to keep from saying more.

"Don't be. I won't let anything happen to you."

"It's not me I'm scared for."

"Melody's going to be okay, too."

"I hope you're right."

"I am."

Tori wished she had his confidence, his faith that everything would work out.

Someone let out a shrill whistle, and the soft hum of the compound became a buzz of activity as teams gathered gear and lined up at the gate.

"It's time." Noah spoke above the noise, his words clipped, tension radiating out of him as he led Tori into the crowd.

Hawke waited at the gate, his eyes eerily light against swarthy skin. A pile of supplies sat in a box beside him, and he reached down to grab a large backpack, handing it to Noah. "Simon is waiting behind the compound with his motorcycle. You and the lady can ride into Samrarn's village. There's a radio in the pack. Check in with news if there is any at the village. If not, check in on the hour and half hour."

"Will do. Where will you and Simon be?"

"I'm due east of your grid section. Simon will be north. Between the three of us, we've got most of the Wa's stronghold. Maybe twenty villages that have been known to work with Lao or his Myanmar friends. If the girl is not in one of them, she is probably not anywhere."

Tori stiffened at his words. "What are you saying?"

"Lao is just as likely to ki—"

"You've said enough, Hawke." Noah's words were quiet, but effective, cutting off Hawke's words before he could say the one thing Tori didn't want to hear—that Melody might already be dead.

Hawke raised an eyebrow, but let the subject drop. "You might want to reconsider taking the lady. The terrain's rough and there is a lot of it to cover."

"Not a possibility. We're together for the duration."

"Your call." Hawke stepped aside, and Noah led Tori through the gate and out into predawn shadows.

Chapter Eleven

Adrenaline hummed along Noah's nerves as he followed the line of the fence to the back of the compound. Several groups had converged there, most heading into the jungle, searching for tracks leading away from the place where the woman's body had been found earlier. They might find some. More than likely, though, any signs that Lao's men had been there had been obliterated by too many feet trampling the underbrush.

Better to pursue other avenues.

Like the information provided by Samrarn. If it was accurate, if it hadn't been embellished or completely contrived, Melody might be within walking distance of the Blue H'mong village where Samrarn lived. It made sense. Noah had spent years traveling the area, and knew of several villages that worked for Lao and for the Wa. Melody might be in one of them, though there was no guarantee they'd find her. No guarantee she was still alive. For now Noah would hope for the best and push forward as if there was every reason to believe the girl would be found.

Simon waited in the shadow of the jungle, a sleek black motorcycle parked beside him, a scowl darkening his tan face. "You wreck my bike and you better hope Lao's men get to you before I do."

"I'll bring it back in one piece."

"One piece isn't what I'm looking for. I'm looking for the same condition it's in now."

"Right. I'll do my best." Noah climbed onto the bike, steadying it as Tori slid on behind him. Her fingers touched his sides, barely grasping the material of his T-shirt.

"Better hold on tighter than that."

"I'm fine."

For now. But Noah decided to let her figure that out herself.

The first few miles were easygoing—smooth, dark pavement sliding under the wheels of the motorcycle with little bounce or bump to it. Soon, though, the glide of wheels over pavement gave way to the harsh thump of the bike traveling over deeply rutted road. Tori gasped and hooked her arms around Noah's waist, her fingers digging into his sides, her breath coming in harsh, fast puffs next to his ear.

"I guess there's no way to avoid the bumps?" The words were almost a shout above the rumble of the engine.

"Sorry."

"How much farther?"

"Maybe fifteen miles."

"What happens when we get there?"

"I'll talk to Samrarn. Check out his story. Maybe talk to some other people in the village. From there, we'll work the grid, visit other villages. If Melody's being held somewhere around here, someone will know."

"But will anyone be willing to admit it?"

"That depends on who knows what. Many of the Blue H'Mong are related. Which means lots of communication between villages. If Melody's being kept nearby, there's probably a general consensus regarding what should be done about it. All we need is one tribal leader willing to talk. The villagers will follow suit."

"Then I guess we'd better hope one of the leaders is willing to talk."

"Hope is good. Prayer is better."

Tori didn't argue with his words, though her own prayers had often gone unanswered. Nor would she spend time wondering about the whys of that. There were more important things to think about—like how they were going to find Melody before the deadline was up. "Think there'll be signs of the men Samrarn heard? Tracks we can follow?"

"It's possible. We look hard enough, we might find something."

"But you don't think so?"

"If I had my dogs with me, yes. But I'm no trained tracker, and the jungle is dense with summer growth. The likelihood that I'll spot something useful is slim."

"You have search dogs?"

"Yeah. I've got three handlers on my team, as well. It's what I've been doing during my retirement—training service dogs and their handlers. Another few months and I'll be ready to open my own training facility."

"We could use a few of your search dogs right about now."

"Too dangerous. The trainers are civilians. No combat experience. Hold on. Road's turning to dirt."

The motorcycle pitched forward and Tori gasped,

her hands tightening convulsively on Noah's waist, pain spearing through her side. She pushed it away, focusing her attention on the surroundings, wishing some clue would jump out at her, some sign that Melody had been this way. Thick jungle hedged the road, bright red flowers peeking out from deep green foliage. Mosquitoes droned and swarmed above muddy puddles, the stench of rotting leaves hanging in the gray morning mist. Moisture coated the leaves and worked its way through the cotton T-shirt Tori wore. She clenched her jaw against the shivers working their way up her spine and threatening to dislodge her from the motorcycle. A jacket would be nice. Or better still—a cup of cocoa, a warm seat in front of the fireplace at home. The heavy afghan Gran had made for Christmas five years ago.

She didn't realize her eyes had closed until the motorcycle stopped. She jerked her head up, looked around. "Where are we?"

"A couple miles from Samrarn's village. We'll hide the bike and walk in from here."

Tori bit back a groan as she hopped off the bike, her body stiff and uncooperative, her hands and legs uncoordinated as she worked with Noah to push the bike into deep undergrowth and cover it with foliage.

"Good enough. Let's go."

By the time they reached the village, stilt-legged huts were clearly visible, their thatched roofs black in still-dim morning light. Ten houses in all, the huts formed a semicircle, the fenced areas beneath each containing odd assortments of animals and fowl scratching at the dirt in search of early-morning food.

"*Sawatdee khrap!*" The cheerful greeting sliced through the silence, the man who issued it hurrying down the stairs of the hut closest to the road, his spindly legs and spare torso made obvious by the traditional costume he wore—loose cotton pants that fell just past his knees and a colorful silk blouse.

"*Sawatdee khrap.* Are you Samrarn?"

"Yes. Yes."

"Noah Stone. This is Tori Riley."

Tori smiled, accepted the man's handshake and then mimicked his deep bow.

"Welcome. Come please." He led the way up the stairs to his hut, his movements quick and light. Then he slipped off his shoes and gestured them inside.

Noah kicked off his shoes, motioned for Tori to do the same and then followed. The room they stepped into was as spare as its owner—the wood floor covered with woven rugs, a loom taking center stage. A wizened Thai woman sat in front of the loom, rising as Tori and Noah approached.

"My wife. Doom." Samrarn gestured to the woman who bowed deeply before hurrying from the room.

"Sit. We eat."

"No—"

Before she could finish the protest, Noah cut in. "Food would be good. Thank you."

He grabbed Tori's hand and pulled her close, whispering in her ear as he urged her toward a low teak table. "We'll get the information we need a lot faster if we accept his hospitality."

"And waste more time? You eat. I'll go look around the village."

"You'll do things my way. Just like you promised." His voice was hard, brooking no argument.

Tori would have argued anyway if Samrarn weren't

watching with dark, curious eyes. He said something in Thai, the lilting tone of the words belying the seriousness of his gaze.

"He asked if you want medicine for your bruises."

"No. I'm all right. Thank you." She met Samrarn's eyes, saw pity in the depth of his gaze and turned away, easing onto a rough-hewn chair that sat in front of the table. The air in the hut was cool and scented with curry, the open windows letting in moisture and the chatter and chirp of jungle animals rising to greet the day.

Noah settled into the chair beside Tori, speaking to Samrarn in Thai, his tones and inflections indistinguishable from native Thais Tori had heard. Samrarn responded, a frown line appearing between his brow. The conversation heated, words flying fast and furious. Tori had no hope of understanding what was being said, though the tension in both men was obvious. Neither looked up as the woman reentered the room, or acknowledged her as she set a tray on the table.

Tori looked up, saw that Doom was watching her, deep brown eyes flashing with intelligence and interest.

"You eat." She slid a bowl of what looked to be rice soup in front of Tori.

"Thank you." Tori's hand shook as she sank a spoon into the bowl and shoveled up a mouthful of spicy soup.

"Tea." Doom gestured to tiny cups sitting on the tray.

Tori nodded, accepted one of the cups and took a sip of the bitter brew.

Noah and Samrarn were eating, as well, their conversation punctuated by the tap of spoons against bowls and the clink of teacups on the tray.

Wasting time.

Tori set the spoon down beside her bowl, the thought of taking another bite when Melody might be hungry and scared making her stomach churn. What was taking so long? What could the two men possibly be discussing?

She thought Noah too intent on the conversation to notice her agitation, but he grabbed her hand, gave it a gentle squeeze, his thumb rubbing back and forth along her knuckles in a gesture meant to soothe.

After what seemed a lifetime, Samrarn stood, his brows furrowed, his smile gone. He hurried from the room and Noah turned to Tori, still clasping her hand in his. "He might know where Melody's being held."

"Then what are we waiting for?" She jumped up, dizzy with the swiftness of the motion.

"Not so fast, Red." Noah stood, too, his grip on Tori's hand holding her in place when she would have raced after Samrarn.

"If he knows—"

"*Might* know. He says he's got a cousin who lives near the Myanmar border. Cousin's been known to traffic for Lao. Could be that's where Lao's men were heading."

"Then why are we standing here? If she's there, the sooner we get to her the better."

"We're waiting for Samrarn's brother. I agreed to let him go ahead of us. Convince the cousin that Samrarn needs his help. Get him out of there in case there's trouble."

"We should go now. Melody's an innocent who's done nothing wrong. Samrarn's cousin is a drug runner. If he's in the middle of trouble, it's because he chooses to be." She started moving again, but Noah pulled her back.

"I was given the location of the village in exchange for my word that Samrarn's brother would have an hour's head start. I won't break that trust."

"You won't have to. I will."

"I'm afraid I can't let you do that."

"So you'd rather let Samrarn's brother warn the village that we're on the way? Let them have the chance to move Melody to another location?"

"We've got no reason to believe he'll do that."

"We've got no reason to believe he won't."

"Always the cynic, Red."

"So you're saying you haven't thought about it? That you haven't considered that that might be exactly what Samrarn's brother is going to do?"

"To what end?"

She had no answer to that, though her pulse raced with the need to go after Samrarn, to follow his brother to the village where Melody might be. "I don't know. I'm just not sure I trust either man."

"Is there anyone you do trust?" He spoke quietly, but the question resounded through the room.

Did she trust anyone? Maybe Pops. The Raymonds. But even with them she was careful to show only part of what she felt, say part of what she thought. No. She didn't trust anyone. Not really. And maybe not even herself.

She pulled away from Noah's hand, stalked across the room to stare out the open window. "Trust isn't something I do easily. Neither is waiting."

"Why doesn't that surprise me?" He leaned against the doorjamb, relaxed and at ease.

"How can you be so calm?"

"The truth? I'm not. I want out of here, too."

"So let's go."

"Like I said before, I gave my word. I'm not going to break it. Besides, you're done in. Maybe waiting a while is for the best."

"It's not like I'll be resting while we wait."

"No, but waiting might give you time to change your mind about coming with me."

"What do you mean? I thought we were joined at the hip until this was over."

"Not if one of us can't make it to the next village."

"I can make it."

"Can you?"

"I said I can."

Noah straightened, pushing away from the wall and walking toward Tori with the same long, powerful stride she'd noticed the first time she'd seen him. He leaned toward her, staring into her eyes so intently she fidgeted.

"What?"

"It's a long hike into the jungle, Tori. And it's not just the bad guys you have to worry about. There are snakes, spiders, rats as big as cats. Plants with spines so sharp they'll go through to the bone. The terrain is rough, the route we're taking no more than a footpath. Sometimes less than that. And there's no guarantee Melody will be in the village once we get there."

"If you're trying to scare me, it won't work. I passed scared days ago." But her heart was thumping with anxiety, her body begging her to stay put.

"Not scare. Warn. We've got a rough day ahead. If you've got any doubt you can make it, stay here. Samrarn and his wife would be happy to have you."

"I can make it."

Could she? Noah wasn't sure. Nor was he sure that

leaving her behind was wise. The woman who had the guts to run from the DEA wouldn't hesitate to run from Samrarn and his wife. Not if it meant finding her daughter. "It's your choice. This time. But remember what you agreed to—you'll do what I say, when I say it, no questions. If you don't, you could be risking your life and Melody's."

She nodded, her eyes wide with anxiety, her hands tight fists. One foot tapped a quick beat on the wood floor, and her pulse jumped at the base of her throat. Nervous. Good. She should be. The mountains of Mae Hong Son weren't a place for carelessness. Even after years spent traveling the depth of the jungle, Noah had a healthy respect and instinctive caution toward the pristine wilderness.

Which was why he was worried about Tori.

She didn't look capable of walking a city block, let alone twenty miles of backcountry trails. Of course, if he judged by looks alone he wouldn't have believed her capable of leaping a five-foot chasm and dropping twenty feet into his arms. She'd managed it. Just as he suspected she'd manage whatever the next few hours would bring.

"You're staring at me like I'm a bug under a microscope."

"Am I? Sorry." He stretched, felt the muscles in his shoulder and back protest. "I'm going to see if Samrarn's brother is on his way. The sooner we get moving, the happier I'll be."

"I'll come with you."

"Not this time."

She opened her mouth, then snapped it shut again, pressing her lips together and taking a deep breath before she spoke. "How long will you be?"

"Not long." He pushed the door open, would have walked out into the silver light of dawn, but Tori spoke, her voice so quiet, he almost didn't hear.

"Are you really coming back?"

He turned, more surprised by her tone than by the question.

She'd looked vulnerable, the deep gashes on her wrists crimson lines against white skin. The bruises on her face had darkened over the past few hours, and her cheek seemed painted in rainbow hues, but it was her eyes that caught and held Noah's attention. Dark brown, framed by thick lashes, they should have shown little of what she felt. Instead they showed everything—fear, doubt, worry and the quiet strength that kept her going.

He brushed a strand of hair back behind her ear, letting his fingers linger for a moment. "Yeah. I'm coming back."

He didn't bother saying more, just stepped outside, praying that the next few days wouldn't hurt Tori more than she'd already been, that *he* wouldn't hurt her more than she'd already been hurt.

Chapter Twelve

The door closed with a quiet click, and Tori slumped down onto a chair, her head aching with fatigue, her mind numb with fear and worry. Both wrists throbbed with pain so intense she knew they were infected. Each deep breath sent a knife through her side. She grimaced, shifting in the chair and trying to make herself more comfortable. It didn't work. Nor did wrapping her arms around her waist stop the shivers that coursed through her. Fever or fear or maybe the morning chill. Whatever the cause, her bones ached with cold, her teeth chattering so hard she clenched her jaw.

Good thing Noah didn't know how she felt. If he did, he'd tie her up and leave her here rather than let her venture into the jungle. Not that she was convinced he actually planned to take her with him. For all she knew, he had no intention of coming back. She glanced at the door, imagining Noah hurrying down the steps, rushing into the jungle and away from the village.

"No. He said he'd be back."

As if that meant anything. Hadn't Melody's father

told Tori the same? Even now, thirteen years later, she could still hear his voice, still see the sincerity in his eyes when he told her he'd come back once he had his degree. She'd been fifteen, eager to believe their yearlong relationship would last forever. But Matt hadn't come back. Not when she'd written to him, sending the letter care of MIT, not when she'd hitchhiked to Massachusetts and stood in his dorm, begging him to do what he'd said he would—marry her. His laughter had been a much crueler blow than a simple rejection might have been.

Tori shook her head against the memory, forcing herself to stand, to move across the room, to stare out the window into the brightening day. The past was just that, past. She'd made her mistakes. She'd paid for them. She hoped. Another chill swept along her arms, and she shivered again, refusing to think that what was happening now was payback for the sins she'd committed. God wasn't that cruel, that vindictive. Was He?

"Cold, yes?"

Tori whirled toward the voice, her muscles relaxing as she spotted Doom. Curved back, concave chest, skinny arms covered from forearm to elbow with bracelets, she watched Tori with a mixture of compassion and curiosity. "You cold. Yes?"

"I'm okay."

The woman shook her head, the vigorous movement causing tiny bells on her hat to chime. "Too cold. No good. You come."

Tori didn't resist when the woman grabbed her hand and tugged her across the room, pulling her into what could only be a bedroom. A large mattress lay on the floor, made neatly and covered with a Thai silk spread.

On one side of it, a dresser fit snug against the wall. The woman hurried toward it, tugged open a drawer and pulled out a neatly folded cloth. She shook it open, letting it unfold into a poncho woven in black and deep red, the craftsmanship stunning, the design so intricate Tori couldn't imagine the hours spent creating it.

"For you."

"Oh no, I couldn't."

"For you." She emphasized the words by thrusting the cloth toward Tori, a smile showing a gaping space where one front tooth should be.

"Thank you. You're very kind."

"Doom." She patted her chest, smiling again as Tori slid the poncho over her head and let the heavy wool drop around her shoulders and arms.

"I'm Tori."

"You sit now."

"I'm fine."

"No. Sit. Come." Her English was limited, but the older woman had definite ideas about what she wanted, leading Tori back out into the main room and gesturing to the chair. "Sit. Rest."

"My friend will be back soon." But she sat anyway, letting the thick wool of the poncho fall over her knees, encasing her in warmth.

Doom smiled approval as she gathered soup bowls and cups onto a tray. The gentle clink of earthenware and utensils reminded Tori of home. She closed her eyes, imagining she was there and that Pops was cooking breakfast—thick slabs of bacon and bright yellow eggs, served with strong black coffee. She let her mind wander, her eyes still closed, her muscles heavy and finally warm.

Was Melody warm? Safe? Or was she cold and scared, alone and wondering when someone would come to bring her home?

Where was Noah?

Shouldn't he be back by now?

Was he actually coming back?

Questions flew through her mind one after another, and she opened her eyes again, her heart racing with worry and fear. She'd give Noah a few more minutes, then she'd go look for him.

And if she didn't find him? What then?

Would she find her way back to Mae Hong Son? Wander into the jungle and try to find Melody on her own? Ask someone to take her to the next village?

None of the options appealed to her; none seemed feasible. That didn't mean she wouldn't try. She'd just take her time, think through her choices and then act. Just as she'd done when her stepfather had kicked her out of the house, leaving her homeless and three months pregnant. Just as she'd done when Matt had laughed at her futile attempt to coax him into marriage. Just as she'd done when she'd been fifteen, a new mother without a baby to love, and a million dreams for her life, dreams that seemed like they'd never come true.

Now was no different than any of those times.

She'd think things through, make plans, implement those plans.

And hope that everything worked out.

A soft breeze wafted through cracks in the bamboo wall, and the cold that Tori had rid herself of returned. She clenched her jaw against the tremors, wrapped the poncho more tightly around her arms. Jungle sounds drifted in on the breeze, screeches and screams of animals, the noises of life and of death and of struggle.

And then something else. A sharp crack that rent the air, silencing the animals. Tori leaped to her feet, heart slamming against her ribs, her throat tight with fear.

"Come. Come." Doom rushed toward the door, grabbed Tori's shoes.

Tori ran to her side. "What is it? What's wrong?"

"Come. Come." She led her into the bedroom, pulled open a door and pointed to a tiny space crammed tight with clothes. "Up. See."

She patted a thick wood shelf at the top of the closet.

"What? What do you want me to do?"

"Go up. Hurry."

The sound of harsh voices drifted into the room from below. Someone was coming. From Doom's frantic expression, that someone wasn't welcome.

Tori pulled herself up onto the shelf. Four feet long and three feet wide, it wasn't long enough to stretch out on. The ceiling just above Tori's head offered no hope of escape.

This wasn't good. It wasn't good at all.

"You lay." Doom's words were an urgent whisper and Tori obeyed, sliding down onto her side so that she faced the front of the closet. If she were going to face death, she might as well do it head-on. She pressed close to the back wall, praying that whoever was coming wouldn't look into the closet, knowing her prayers were probably useless.

Instead of closing the closet door, Doom hurried to the bed, pulled several colorful pillows from it and piled them around Tori. Next, she grabbed yards of colorful fabric from a box and draped Tori from head to toe with Thai silk.

As camouflage went, it didn't seem like it would be very effective. Head covered, Tori couldn't see the rest of what Doom was doing, though she could feel the heavy weight of more fabric being laid over her and hear the panicky gasp of Doom's breath as she hurried to complete her task.

It took only seconds, but seemed an eternity. Tori could see nothing, could hear nothing but the sloshing hum of her pulse. The silence, after the moments of panicked activity, seemed eerie.

She'd just begun to relax, just begun to think she and Doom had imagined the danger, when a door banged open, the sound thundering through the silence. Tori jumped, then stiffened, ears straining, eyes staring at thick, green silk as if she might see through it to whatever danger approached.

Someone shouted in Thai, the words harsh and angry. Doom's reply was calm, if a bit shaky, her voice barely audible above the riotous thrum of Tori's fear. The click of hard-soled shoes on wood planks brought the first speaker closer to the closet and Tori closer to discovery. She held her breath, wondering if she looked like a lump of fabric or like what she was—a person trying to hide out in the open. She willed her body to stillness, willed her muscles to stop trembling.

Minutes passed, conversation flowing rapidly, tones softening. Someone laughed and shoes tapped against the floor again, the sound fading. Going back into the main room? Tori wasn't sure, so she remained frozen in place, endless seconds ticking by, the soft clink of dishes and steady flow of conversation a backdrop to Tori's racing thoughts.

Where was Noah? Was that a gunshot Tori'd heard

before Doom rushed her into hiding? And where *was* Noah? Her mind circled around to the same thought over and over again, slow dread replacing fear. Had he been shot? Hurt? *Killed?* She wanted to shove out from the fabric that concealed her, race into the room where quiet conversation and soft laughter seemed to mock the seriousness of what was happening.

She wanted to demand answers.

But if she did, she'd be taken again. And if that happened she couldn't expect a second rescue. And what about Melody? She'd be tortured, maybe killed, to convince Tori to hand over the box.

A box Tori no longer had.

They were in trouble. All of them. And Tori could think of no plan, no options she hadn't already thought of, nothing that could be of help to Melody, to Noah or to herself.

What am I going to do?

Her mind scrambled for an idea and came up blank. The urge to pray, to beg God to intervene, was a hot coal in her chest, demanding attention. She ignored it, easing her hand up, shoving aside the fabric that covered her eyes, hoping that clearing her vision would clear her mind.

As if her movement had called back danger, conversation in the other room ceased and the house fell to silence. Not a breath, not a whisper of movement could be heard. Tori inched the cloth back over her face, closed her eyes and did what she should have done minutes ago. She prayed.

Noah watched Samrarn lead his guests out of the hut. They'd been in there a half hour, talking, laughing. Apparently quite sure their quarry was nowhere around. Both men were young, strong and armed to the teeth. Neither seemed in a big hurry to leave. Maybe their hunters' instincts were finally kicking in, telling them their prey was close at hand. If so, they'd keep waiting, keep listening and keep watching until they found what they'd come for. Unfortunately, neither of them would survive the experience.

Noah's gun was a comforting weight in his hand as he slid deeper into the jungle's embrace and crouched low behind thick fronds. From his position, he could see both of Lao's men easily. If he had to, he'd take them down. He didn't want to have to. He wanted the men to go on their way, go back to their boss and report that Tori wasn't anywhere near this village. Let Lao think his secret was safe. It would make rescuing Melody that much easier.

A shout of laughter carried on the morning air as the men descended the stairs and stood in the gloomy shade beneath the hut. Minutes ticked by. Minutes when one wrong move, one wrong word, might lead the two back up to the hut and to Tori. *If* she was still in the hut. Noah shifted his gaze so that he could see the windows at the side of Samrarn's house. The bamboo and thatch design of the structure was perfect for allowing in breezes and keeping out rain. It wasn't so good at concealing movement inside. He watched intently, looking for any sign that Tori was there, but saw nothing. If she was in the hut, she was well hidden. Noah could only pray she'd stay that way. If she grew impatient, if she moved before Lao's men did, there'd be trouble. More than Noah wanted this early in the game.

Ten minutes later the men were gone, heading down

the road, maybe to a ride that waited. Maybe to a better vantage point. Somewhere they could observe the village unnoticed. It was what Noah would do if he were in their place, but they were young and, despite the weapons, had looked nervous. Unless he missed his guess, they were moving as fast as they could, heading back to Lao with a report on what they'd found. Or hadn't found.

In the distance, a howler monkey screeched. Birds sang and cawed, celebrating the birth of the new day. And Noah waited, listening and watching, not moving, barely breathing. Inch by inch his body relaxed, the adrenaline that pumped through him fading. Lao's men were gone. He sensed it as surely as he'd sensed their presence just moments before they'd arrived.

He waited another heartbeat, then rose, easing out of the jungle, his gaze scanning the area, searching for signs of danger. Up the wooden steps to the hut, a quick knock and Doom opened the door, her skin pale and pasty, eyes wide with fear. She didn't speak. Neither did Noah. That they were still in danger was understood, and he followed her into the bedroom, wondering how Tori had stayed hidden in such a small area. One glance around the room told him she wasn't there. The bed was a mattress on the floor, the dresser drawers too small to hide in, the closet door wide open, the interior filled with clothes and cloth, but no tall redhead.

"Where is she?"

"Noah?" A pile of fabric erupted from the closet shelf, falling onto the floor in a heap, revealing red hair and a bruised cheek.

"Talk about hiding in plain sight. Leaving that door open was a stroke of genius." He spoke as he moved toward her, relief at having her safe beating hard in his chest.

"It was Doom's genius, not mine." She pushed green Thai silk from her legs, wincing a little as she shimmied to the edge of the shelf and dropped off.

Noah caught her around the waist, holding her steady as she gained her balance. Her hair smelled of flowers, the soft curls tickling against his chin. He brushed them aside, surprised by the heat of her skin. "You're warm."

"Being smothered under a ton of blankets will do that to a person." She stepped back, smiled, her lips trembling a little. "I'm glad to see you're in one piece. I was getting worried."

"Were you?"

"I thought you'd come running to save me as soon as Lao's men showed up. When you didn't I thought something had happened to you."

"I was just waiting things out. No sense letting Lao know we're here until we're ready."

"So the gunshot wasn't directed at you?"

"It wasn't directed at anyone, just a motivator to get Samrarn moving toward his hut."

"It worked."

"Yeah, but it also warned you that trouble was coming. Lao wouldn't be happy to know how careless his men were."

"Maybe not, but I am." She rubbed a hand along the back of her neck, the colorful poncho she wore a stark contrast to the paleness of her skin.

He wanted to take her back to Chiang Mai, leave her under lock and key. But there wasn't time. Not with Lao's men on the move. "Their rashness bought us some time. As long as Lao doesn't know we're closing in, he won't move Melody. And as long as she's staying in one place, we have a chance of finding her."

"Not if we're sitting here."

"Then we'd better get going. You ready?"

"Of course," she replied, though her legs were trembling so much she wasn't sure she could walk across the room, let alone make her way through the jungle.

Noah eyed her for a moment, then pulled open the door and stepped outside. "Let's go."

Tori followed him, her body shaking with cold and fear as she made her way down the steps.

Chapter Thirteen

The cool morning air held a hint of moisture, the ground beneath Tori's feet giving off the loamy scent of decaying plants. With every step, the jungle closed in, cutting them off from civilization. A million eyes could be watching from the depth of the jungle and Tori wouldn't know it. She shuddered, glanced back, caught a glimpse of Samrarn's village and had the urge to run back, hide under the pile of cloth and pillows again. Of course, she wouldn't. She'd stick things out until the end. No matter what the end might be.

Right now she was pretty sure it wouldn't be good.

Noah moved quickly despite his sleepless night—immune to fatigue, to fear, to all the things that plagued Tori. Her feet dragged with each step, her breath hissed out in gasps as thorns and twigs pierced through jeans and into flesh. Worse were the stabbing pain in her side and throbbing ache in her wrists. Only the knowledge that Melody was waiting for rescue kept her moving forward.

Sunlight dappled through thick leaves, sprinkling the ground with hazy light. The mist that had seemed innocuous in the village layered the jungle floor—a living thing that swirled around Tori's ankles. Mosquitoes swarmed around her, driven to a frenzy by the scent of blood. Tori didn't have the energy to swat them away. Her focus was on the ground—the vines and roots threatening to trip her.

She didn't notice Noah had stopped. Not until she walked into his back.

She tumbled, scrambling for balance, her arms reaching for leverage and finding Noah's shirt. She caught the material, gasping as he grabbed her wrist to hold her steady.

"Everything okay?" He turned to meet her gaze, his hand falling away.

She blinked back tears of pain, nodded without speaking.

"Do you need to stop for a few minutes?"

"Not yet. Let's keep moving." She didn't add that if they stopped she wasn't sure she'd ever start again.

"You sure? The next few miles will be rough."

"I'm sure." She stepped up beside him, her heart skittering in her chest as she saw the reason he'd stopped. A deep ravine cut into the mountain in front of them. A hundred feet below a sliver of blue shimmered through the mist.

She tried to make her voice sound confident. "Now what?"

"We cross. See that fallen tree?" He gestured to the left, and Tori saw a large tree that had fallen across the ravine. Leaves still green, branches jutting out on every side, it bridged the divide but didn't look like the safest means of forging the chasm. Not that she could see any other choices.

"I see it. I'm just not sure I want to use it as a bridge."

"It's that or spend an extra couple of hours trying to find a way around."

"Right. So who goes first?"

He eyed her a moment, his steady gaze seeming to take in more than she wanted it to. "I'll go. Make sure it'll hold my weight before you try."

"But—"

"Let's not waste time arguing." He smiled, flashing white teeth, though his eyes were anything but happy.

"Fine. Just be careful."

His expression softened, his fingers linking through hers as he pulled her a few steps closer to the tree. "See the midway point?"

"Yeah."

"Wait until I get past it and then follow."

He said it as if he were telling her to follow him across a street, or along a sidewalk rather than onto a tree stretched across a wide gorge.

Noah moved onto the tree with ease, and Tori waited until he passed the halfway point before stepping on behind him. The trunk seemed smaller when she was standing on it, the bark peeling, branches sticking up and out to either side. Below, the sliver of water was indistinct, meandering through mist-shrouded foliage.

"I'm not so sure about this." She didn't realize she'd spoken aloud until Noah responded, his voice carrying above the sound of Tori's pounding heart.

"Take your time. There's no hurry."

Maybe not in Noah's mind, but Tori's mind was screaming that she'd better get herself across the chasm. Fast!

She took a quick step forward, wanting to close the

space between herself and Noah. Took another step, telling herself not to look down. And that's when she saw it. Bright green head, forked tongue. A tree viper. She'd seen pictures of them, watched animal handlers talk about them on educational programs, but had never had a close-up look at one. She would have preferred to save the experience for another day.

"Snake," she whispered, as though the snake could hear her.

Noah eased around to face her, his gaze dropping to the viper. "Don't panic."

"Easy for you to say. He's not looking at you."

"Just stay still." There was tension in his voice as he snapped a branch from the tree and took a step closer.

"Be careful. It's turning."

"I'm on it." One quick movement of the stick sent the snake flying into the gorge. "Okay, let's move out."

He turned, walking away as if nothing had happened, and Tori followed.

Afterwards Tori could never say exactly how it happened. One minute she was taking another step, the next she was falling, arms flying out, legs tangled together. The world tilted. The chasm beneath, a hodgepodge of color and texture—greens and grays, rocks and water.

Something snagged Tori's poncho, slowing her fall but not stopping it. Her hands grasped at wood, splinters forcing their way into her palms as she struggled for purchase. She was sliding, slipping off the log, her fingernails digging into wood and bending back.

A hand slammed over hers, then grabbed her wrists, the pain from the contact so sharp, a million stars danced in front of her eyes.

"No!" Noah's voice cracked like gunfire, clearing the fog in Tori's head.

She struggled to focus, saw his face inches from hers, his eyes clear green-blue.

"I'm okay. I'm okay."

"You're right. Now keep your eyes open and focus. We're not in a good position here." The words were sharp, and Tori noticed just how precarious things were.

She dangled over the chasm, Noah's grip on her wrists the only thing keeping her from falling into it. He lay on his stomach, his head and arms hanging over the log.

"I'm focused."

"Good. Here's what we're going to do. I'm going to pull you up. You're going to do what you can to help me." With that he yanked hard and she bit her lip against the pain in her arms, a pain that was nothing compared to what she would feel if she slammed down onto the earth below.

"Get ready to swing your leg over the top." Noah's grip on one wrist loosened and his hand brushed against her back. He grabbed the waistband of her jeans and tugged hard enough to give her the leverage she needed. She swung her leg up and over the wood and lay there panting.

"Okay?" Noah smoothed the hair from Tori's face, his hand trembling just a little.

She nodded, unable to force words of reassurance past the tightness in her throat.

"Good. Let's go." He pushed to his feet, balancing effortlessly, his legs planted, one hand extended toward her.

She grabbed it, using her free hand to push up.

"That's it. Take your time. We're almost there." He stared into her eyes as if willing his own calm into her, then started forward again.

Tori forced herself to do the same, taking one wobbling step after another, refusing to look beyond the thick tree trunk she balanced on. Sweat beaded her brow and slid into her eyes. She wiped it away, the poncho that had warmed her earlier suddenly a weight that threatened to drag her into the chasm. By the time she reached the far side of the gorge, she was gasping for breath, her lungs heaving as if she'd run a marathon.

Noah grabbed her as she stumbled off the trunk, his arms wrapping around her in a hug that threatened to break her already-bruised ribs. "That was a little too close."

She nodded against his chest, the wild thump of her heart slowing to match the steady beat of his. "You saved my life, you know. This is the second time. No, the third."

"Who's counting?"

"Me."

"Don't." He loosened his grip, tipped her chin up with his finger.

Tori's stomach lurched, her pulse leaping. Everything in her stilled as she realized what she was feeling—attraction; she thought she'd outgrown it long ago.

She jerked back, stepping away from the warmth of Noah's chest, the comfort of his arms. "Don't what? Keep track? I have to. I always pay back what I owe."

Fear made her voice sharper than she intended, and Noah must have noticed.

His eyes narrowed, his mouth pulling into a hard line. "You don't owe me anything. I'm doing a job. Keeping you safe is part of it."

"Is it? I thought you were being paid to get the box and the information it contained."

"That's what I'm getting paid for, but it's not my only responsibility. I told your grandfather I'd get you home safe. That's what I plan to do. Come on. The clock is ticking and we're getting nowhere fast." He started away from the gorge, leading Tori into ever deepening jungle.

Trees towered above, thick vines and rotting stumps gnarled the ground. The air seemed to close in around Tori, stealing her breath. Noah seemed impervious to the heat and humidity as he pushed through the foliage, heading toward a village that lay somewhere ahead. Though how he would find it through the prison of trees Tori didn't know. "How much farther?"

"A few miles."

"'A few' as in three, or 'a few' as in ten?"

"Does it matter?" He glanced back, and Tori straightened her spine trying to look less tired than she felt.

"No."

"Then you're better off not knowing."

"And if Melody isn't there when we arrive?"

"Then we keep searching until we find her."

"You always sound so confident."

"I always am confident."

"Even when things look impossible?"

"Nothing is impossible, Red. Not even things that look like they are."

Maybe for someone like Noah the impossible became possible with a prayer, or whatever it was that led him through the jungle with such unerring precision. But for Tori impossibilities existed and she was beginning to think getting out of the jungle might be one of them. "Are you sure we're heading in the right direction. Everything looks the same."

"I'm sure."

"But—"

"We've got a steep climb ahead. Better conserve your energy for that."

"That would be easier to do if I were sure we weren't walking around in circles."

"We're not."

"And you know this because?"

"I've traveled this way a dozen times. Probably more."

"Doing what? Sneaking through the jungle and catching bad guys who were carrying drugs across the border?"

He held a thick, spiny branch back, motioning for her to move past, then stepped in front of her again. "Not quite."

"Now I'm intrigued."

Intrigued? She sounded more tired than anything. But pointing that out wouldn't do either of them any good. Instead Noah gave her the distraction she seemed to want. "I was undercover, working as a courier for the Wa. I'd probably still be doing it if I hadn't been injured."

"Was your cover blown? Is that how you were injured?"

"No."

"So what happened?"

Telling her seemed easier than changing the subject, so he shrugged, pulled a bottle of water from his pack, passing it back to Tori before he spoke. "I'd been in the Wa for five years, working my way closer to the head of the organization. General Jittanart Punnok was a hard man with few friends, but he trusted me—thought I was an ex-patriot, running from murder and drug charges. Because of that, he picked me to carry out a special assignment. He suspected one of his chemists was selling information to the Royal Thai Police and he wanted him dead."

"Just because he suspected the man?"

"I told you he was a hard man. Besides, the chemist *was* passing information, but not to the police. To the DEA."

"He must have known Punnok would find out."

"You're right. Ganjan knew, but he was willing to risk getting caught for what the DEA was offering—safe passage to the States for him and for his family. All Ganjan had to do was supply names of the drug cartel working in Bangkok and Chiang Mai. Unfortunately, getting that information wasn't easy, and before he could complete the assignment Punnok got wise to him. That's when I was told to make the hit."

"But you didn't."

"No. I contacted my supervisor, told him I planned to escort Ganjan and his family across the border into Thailand. Wasted a few days getting confirmation of the plan. By the time I was ready to make my move, Punnok's son, Jaran, had decided to take matters into his own hands. He went to Ganjan's house the morning I was supposed to carry out the assassination. By the time I got there Ganjan was dead. So was his six-year-old daughter."

"I'm so sorry."

"Me, too. But sorry doesn't change what happened. It doesn't bring back Ganjan or his daughter. It doesn't heal the sorrow of the wife and mother left behind."

"So his wife survived?"

"Yes. When I arrived, Jaran had a gun to her head. I stopped him before he could pull the trigger."

"She was lucky."

"There's no such thing as luck, Red. Let's stop here."

Tori was so caught up in the story Noah was telling that she didn't register the last few words until she walked into his back. "Sorry."

He wrapped an arm around her waist, smiling slightly as he plucked the water bottle from her hand. "I'm getting used to it."

He took a deep swallow of water, wiping moisture from his lip and offering the bottle back to Tori. "Want more?"

"No." She leaned back against a tree and watched through fatigue-bleary eyes as Noah used his radio to check in with Hawke.

She waited until he slipped the radio back into his pack before asking about Melody. "Any news?"

"None. But it's still early on."

Early on? Hours had passed since Melody had been taken. Hours when anything could have happened to her. But Tori couldn't think about that. Not if she wanted to keep moving, keep believing that Melody would be found whole and healthy. She forced herself away from the tree. "Then we'd better keep moving."

He nodded, taking his place in front of her again. Strong, sure. He didn't look like he'd ever been injured, ever been forced to leave his job because of it.

"You never told me how you were injured."

"Jaran's friends put two bullets in me before I could stop them."

Stop them as in killed them? Tori didn't ask the question. All she had to do was remember the moment she'd first seen Noah to know what he was capable of. "I guess you were lucky, too."

He stopped short, turning to face her. "Like I said before, there's no such thing as luck. Just hard work, persistence. And grace."

"Grace? I'm not sure I know what that means."

"No?"

"I—"

"Shhh." Noah placed a finger against Tori's lips and leaned close to her ear. "Listen."

She did, suddenly noticing what she hadn't before—the silence of the jungle, the absence of bird songs and animal calls.

"It's quiet," she whispered past lips gone dry with fear.

"Too quiet." His words barely stirred the air near her ear. "Let's move."

Tori's heart slammed against her ribs, and her legs shook with unspent adrenaline as they eased into thick foliage. Noah tugged at her hand, urging her down. She lay flat, large-leafed ferns covering her. She might have burrowed deeper into their shadowy embrace, but Noah's arm slipped across her back, holding her still.

Sounds drifted on the still air. The soft pad of feet on dirt and grass, a whisper of fabric, the murmur of voices. Not forest creatures going about their lives. Men. Stalking human prey. And they were coming closer.

Noah's hand slid up her arm, then cupped her jaw, urging her face toward his. He was so close she could feel the warmth of his breath against her cheek, the tension of his muscles. She could see the gun in his free hand, the determination in his eyes.

"Don't move. Don't even breathe heavy, understand?" He mouthed the words and she did the same with her response.

The voices drew closer, the pad of feet louder. Then both slowly faded away. After several minutes, the jungle sprang to life again. Only then did Noah stand up and offer Tori a hand. "We've lost more time. You ready to move fast?" His voice was low, barely audible.

"What about the people who just passed?"

"Not looking for us. If they were, they'd have come a lot more quietly."

That should have been comforting. It wasn't. Tori imagined men sliding through the jungle, stalking her, attacking when she least expected it. She shivered, pulling the poncho tighter.

"Scared?"

"Terrified."

"If you weren't, I'd be worried. Fear keeps a person cautious and alive." He smiled, a half grin that reminded Tori of home, its easy warmth comforting and comfortable, as if he were an old friend sharing a private joke.

But, of course, he wasn't. He was a man she'd known less than two days. A man who made her long for what she could never have again—the ability to trust someone else, to believe in a person's goodness. To hope.

She turned away from him, not wanting to be pulled into Noah's smile, or into her own foolish wish that he was exactly what he seemed to be—a man of strength, integrity and warmth. "You're too good to be true, Noah Stone."

The words were barely a whisper, but Noah heard.

"I'm no different than any other man." He put his hands on Tori's shoulders, felt fragile bones and strong muscles as he urged her back around.

There was fear in her eyes, and a longing she must have wanted desperately to hide. "Any other man I've known would have gone running the minute he realized how much trouble I was in."

"Then you haven't known the right men."

"That's true. All I've known are the wrong men."

"So maybe it's time to change things." His hand rested against her neck, her pulse beating against his palm.

She shifted beneath his touch, a frown line between her brows. "It's *time* to find Melody. That's all I can worry about right now." But her voice shook as she said it, and Noah knew she felt what he did—an interest that couldn't be denied. Eventually they'd both have to face it.

For now he'd let her have the space she needed.

He let his hand slide away from her neck and turned north. "This will be rough going. Stay close. If you need to stop, let me know."

"I will."

She wouldn't. In the short time he'd known her, Noah had learned that about Tori—she never gave up. She'd push forward until she dropped. Then she'd pull herself up and go again.

But there would come a time when she wouldn't be able to pull herself up. Eventually the fatigue that danced at the corners of her eyes would overwhelm her and she wouldn't be able to go on. Noah could only pray they'd make it to Melody before that happened.

He kept the pace slow and steady, pushing aside vegetation, lending a hand as Tori picked her way over fallen logs and through tangled brambles. She never complained, never slowed, just kept moving behind him, her breath gasping out, her feet shuffling through the endless vegetation as they moved up the steep slope of the mountain.

Chapter Fourteen

By noon the jungle was sweltering, humidity rising from the carpet of decaying leaves in waves. Sunlight filtered through the canopy, bathing the trees in hazy light. Noah shoved aside thick vines and pushed forward, ignoring the sting of sweat in his eyes and the ache in his shoulder. Worry spurred him on, the harsh rasp of Tori's breath telling him what she wouldn't—she needed to stop, not for a minute or an hour, but for days.

Unfortunately, they had miles to go before they reached the village, and even then, Noah wasn't sure they'd be at the end of their journey. He prayed they'd find Melody there. If not, they had more villages to search.

Too many more.

Tori was fading fast. So was the day.

Noah pulled the radio from his belt and called in. Still no news. He hadn't expected any. His gut said Melody was within the perimeter of the grid section he was working. All he had to do was find her.

"I could use some more water." Tori's voice was gritty and thick, as if she'd sweated out all the moisture she had in her.

"Let's take a fifteen-minute breather."

"We don't have fifteen minutes."

She was right. Noah wouldn't deny it. But he couldn't deny that Tori was nearing collapse, either. "We're taking fifteen."

"Melody—"

"Drink. Then we'll talk." He stopped, handed a bottle of water to Tori.

She took a long swallow, her hand shaking enough to make the water splash onto the poncho she wore. "I'm ready."

"I said fifteen minutes. Not seconds." He pulled a banana from the pack, handed it to her. "Eat this."

She didn't argue, just peeled the fruit and took a bite. Deep red hair clung to her forehead and cheeks, wild curls blanketing her shoulders. The poncho she wore looked wilted and heavy, the fabric clinging to her arms. Heat and exertion had stained her cheeks deep red, and her eyes were glassy and bright.

"You're overheated. Have some more water and take off the poncho."

"Will it fit in your pack?"

"It's going to have to. We don't want to leave any evidence we've been here."

She pulled it off, folding it neatly before handing it to him. "That's better. Let's go."

"We took ten. Another five won't hurt."

"Yeah, well, it won't help, either, so we may as well head out."

"Determination will only get you so far, Red."

"Let me worry about that. You just worry about getting us to Melody."

Easier said than done.

Noah didn't bother saying as much, just grabbed the water bottle and chugged what was left of it before shrugging back into his pack and taking the lead again. He'd give Tori another hour, a few more miles. Then see how she was faring. If worse came to worst, he'd call Simon in, have him wait with Tori while Noah finished the search.

"I know what you're thinking."

"Do you?" He glanced back, saw her stumble as she stepped over a moss-covered log and put out a hand to stop her fall.

"Yeah. You're thinking I can't make it. That I'm going to slow you down."

"Close enough."

"Well, you can stop thinking it. I'll keep up with you, and I won't stop until we find Melody."

"The sooner the better. For Melody and for you."

She didn't respond, and he knew that she was focusing her energy on keeping up with him.

Within minutes, Tori stumbled over another fallen tree, her foot catching on a root and sending her sprawling. She landed hard, the breath rushing from her lungs, her body throbbing with the impact.

Stunned, she lay still, trying to catch her breath.

Noah crouched down beside her, brushing hair from her cheek, peering into her eyes. "Anything broken?"

"No." She forced herself up, swiping moss and dead leaves from her jeans and grimacing when she saw the dirt embedded in the wounds on her wrists.

"Let's take another breather."

"We could take a hundred breathers and it wouldn't do me any good. I know it, and so do you. We just need to keep going until we get there." She started walking, aiming in the direction they'd been going before her fall. All she had to do was make it to the village. The rest would be easy. Step into the midst of the villagers and let them take her to Lao and to Melody.

But Noah put a hand on her arm, pulling her back. "Tori—"

"Do you have any family, Noah?"

"Three brothers, a sister. Ten nieces and nephews. My parents. Uncles. Aunts."

"What would you do if one of them were in the situation Melody's in?"

"I'd move heaven and earth to get them back."

"Then don't ask me to do any less." She started forward again, determined to keep going.

"Hold it." Noah's arm snaked around her waist, pulling her back and around. "You're planning something. What is it?"

"The same thing you're planning."

"Which is what, exactly?" He stared her down, his eyes flashing fire. He looked like what he said he'd once been to the Wa—a murderer, a felon, a man who lived by no law but his own. A man who knew exactly what she was thinking and didn't like it. But he couldn't know, couldn't have any idea what she'd been planning for the past few hours.

She shifted, running a hand through sweat-damp curls. "I'm planning how I can get Melody back."

"*We're* getting Melody back. All the men and women out searching are getting Melody back."

"That's what I meant."

"I don't think so. I think you meant exactly what you said. You're pushing yourself so hard because you're planning to offer yourself as a sacrifice, your life for Melody's, once we find her."

There was no sense lying. He'd see right through her. "That's a little more dramatic than what I had in mind."

"Yeah? So what exactly do you have in mind?" He began moving as he spoke, urging Tori forward, his arm still around her waist, guiding her over the rough terrain. The danger she'd sensed in him gone, replaced by the same calmness that she'd noticed over and over during their journey.

A man to be counted on?

She didn't dare believe it.

"Well?"

"I thought I could serve as a distraction. Walk into the village where they're keeping Melody. While I've got the attention of Lao's men, you can go in and free Melody."

"And then go back and free you? Sounds like a lot of extra danger for everyone."

"Not if you bring Melody back to Mae Hong Son and let one of the other teams come for me."

"You know there are a million holes in your plan, right?"

"Maybe, but it gets the job done. Melody will be free. We can worry about the rest later."

"Sorry, it doesn't work for me."

"Then how do you propose we get her out?"

"We get to the village. I survey from the perimeter, see if I can get a visual on Melody. If I can verify that's she's there, I'll call in Simon and Hawke. We'll work out a plan, follow it through and have Melody home without risking you."

"And waste the time it will take them to get from wherever they are to us?"

"It isn't a waste if we all get out alive."

He had a point, but Tori still didn't like the idea of waiting any longer than it took to find Melody. "I still think—"

"We had a deal, Red. I'd take you along, you'd do things my way."

"So that means I don't get a say in things?"

"It means that when I come to Lakeview and bring a sick puppy in for treatment, I'll let you decide how to treat him. While we're here, working in an environment I know, doing something I've done for years, you'll let me decide how to handle things."

"Do you always have to make so much sense?"

"Do you ever let other people take control of things?"

"No."

"Then I guess it's good I make so much sense."

Tori couldn't stop the smile that tugged at her lips. She let it have its way, and Noah answered in kind, grinning down at her. "There you go. A smile. I knew you had it in you."

"I smile a lot when I'm not running for my life or trying to rescue someone I love from drug dealers."

"Yeah? Then I guess I'll have to spend some time with you when you're not doing either."

Tori's heart tripped at the thought. Spending time together after this was over was definitely not a good idea. Relying on Noah to help her find Melody was hard enough. Relying on him for friendship, for companionship, for all the things she might expect if they spent too much time together could only lead to heartache.

Keep telling yourself that. Maybe you'll believe it by the time this is over.

"Slope's changing. It's rough going for about a mile. After that, we'll be home free, within a few miles of the village and traveling over easier terrain."

"I can do a rough mile if it means an easier time afterward."

"Let's go then." He slid his arm from around her waist and stepped in front of her, moving easily, despite the hours he'd already spent walking.

Tori followed, her legs like cement logs—ungainly and difficult to move. Despite her brave words, she wasn't sure she could do another mile. Or even half that.

Noah hadn't been lying. The slope was the steepest they'd climbed yet. Tori's lungs heaved, straining for enough oxygen to feed her starved muscles. Sweat poured down her face and neck, but she kept climbing, an image of Melody flashing through her mind and urging her on. Until finally, with one last surge of energy she crested the rise and spotted a nearly dry streambed. From here on, the way should be easier. Tori took a step forward, her legs jerking in spasms, her gaze on Noah's back. He seemed to grow farther away with each breath, the edges of Tori's vision darkening. Then the earth tilted beneath her feet and she was falling.

Chapter Fifteen

"How far are you from the village?" A voice sounded above the static of the radio, filtering through the darkness that Tori wasn't sure she was ready to let go of.

"Three miles."

"So she almost made it. I'm impressed."

"Save your sarcasm for later, Simon. Can you get here, or not?"

"Give me two hours."

"Tell him not to bother. I can make it." She struggled up to a sitting position and decided that was enough for now.

"Change of plans." Noah spoke into the radio but his gaze was on Tori, his eyes hard and angry. "We'll be a mile out. Due east of the village. There's an old hut there. You know it?"

"I'll be there."

Tori waited until Noah clipped the radio back onto his belt before speaking. "You should have told him not to bother."

"We'll meet him on the outskirts of the village. You'll

wait with him until I check things out. If Melody's there, we'll get her. If she's not, Simon will escort you back to the safe house."

She wanted to argue with him. The words danced on the tip of her tongue, begging for release. But she couldn't deny the truth of her physical condition. Just as Noah had said, all the determination in the world wouldn't get her much farther than she'd already come. "Okay."

At her acceptance, Noah's gaze softened, though his lips were still tight. Instead of speaking, he reached into his pack and pulled out a bottle of water. "Drink slow."

She didn't want to drink at all. Her stomach heaved a protest as the first sip of water hit it. "Give me another minute and I'll be ready."

"I could give you a day and you wouldn't be ready." He took the bottle from her hand, wet the edge of the poncho and pressed it against her neck.

The moisture felt cool against her heated skin and she closed her eyes for a minute. "Thanks."

"Why didn't you tell me how bad off you were before we left Mae Hong Son?" The words were soft, though anger simmered beneath them.

She opened her eyes, saw that he was inches away. "I thought I could make it. I really did."

"That's not what I mean, and you know it."

"I don't think I do."

"When I turned you over, your shirt hiked up. You've got bruises on your side and your stomach."

"A few. Nothing serious."

"Out of respect for you, I didn't check to see how much damage there was, but I don't believe there are just a few bruises. And I'm not so sure it isn't serious. So tell me, exactly how bad is it?"

"I don't think anything's broken."

"You don't think? How much bruising?"

"It'd be hard to find a spot that isn't black and blue."

Noah's eyes flashed and he stalked away, hands fisted at his sides. When he turned, he looked like the man she'd first seen—cold, hard and determined to do whatever it took to get what he wanted. "You should be in a hospital, not tracking through the jungle."

"If I'd thought I needed medical attention, I would have had Mark or Joi look me over."

"No. You wouldn't have. Because you were so determined to do things your way, you didn't stop to think of the danger you were putting yourself in. The danger you were putting us all in."

"Wait a minute!" Tori surged up, gasping as sharp pain shot through her side. The fact that Noah stood impassive, watching as she caught her breath, told her just how angry he was. "I didn't put anyone in danger."

"Yeah. You did. Your injuries have slowed us down. Now Simon's being called off the search to escort you back for the medical attention you so clearly need. And what if we find Melody? Are we going to be moving fast when you can't take a deep breath without pain?"

"That isn't fair. I've kept up. Just like I said I would."

"You pushed too hard. Now you've got nothing to give. How is that going to help Melody?"

"I've got plenty left to give."

He ignored her, pacing back toward her, his eyes blazing. "You know what the worst part is?"

She shook her head and swallowed back the lump in her throat.

"The worst part is that you did it because you were

afraid to trust me. You were afraid to believe that I'd do what I said I would. You're so sure you can only count on yourself that you've risked your health, your life and the lives of everyone who's going to have to work to get you back to Mae Hong Son."

"I wasn't thinking of it that way." But maybe she should have been. The knowledge was a hot coal in her chest as Noah shrugged on the pack.

"Let's go."

"I can stay here. I can—"

"Let's go." Noah snapped the command, and if Tori hadn't felt so miserable she would have protested, maybe refused. As it was, she took one shaky step after another, following him down into the streambed and then struggling to climb up the crumbling dirt wall on the other side.

Suddenly, Noah was there, reaching down and grabbing her hand, pulling her up onto solid ground. Then she was in his arms, being held close to his chest, hearing the slow steady beat of his heart. His hand slid down her hair, smoothing it back from her face. "I'm sorry, Red. You didn't deserve my anger."

She shouldn't have been so relieved that he wasn't angry anymore, but she was. Her arms wrapped around his waist, her hands tightening convulsively on his shirt. She wanted to say something, but the words caught in her throat.

"Things are going to work out. You'll see."

She nodded, wishing she could stay where she was for a while longer, but knowing it wasn't possible.

"I know you're worn out, but we've got to keep moving."

When he let his hand slip from her hair and stepped away, Tori forced out the words that needed to be said.

"I'm the one who should be apologizing. Everything you said was true. It would have been better for Melody if I'd stayed in Mae Hong Son."

"What you did, you did out of love for Melody. I can't fault you for that."

"Noah, I—"

"We'll talk more when this is over. Right now, we need to meet Simon and get you and Melody both back home." Noah moved away, anger still clawing at his gut. Not anger at Tori, but anger at the men who'd beaten her so viciously.

He ran a hand down his jaw, wishing he'd had Joi or Mark examine her before they'd left. He'd seen the bruises on her face and neck, the raw wounds on her wrists, and had suspected there were more. But she'd acted fine, giving him trouble at every turn, always on top of things, always working toward her goal. Tough, determined, independent. Until she'd collapsed, he'd thought her gasping breaths were due to fatigue and overexertion. Now he wondered if they were a harbinger of something more serious.

He let his gaze wander back toward her. She seemed oblivious to his scrutiny, her focus on the ground and on putting one foot in front of the other, moving forward even when she must want to collapse onto the ground again.

"We'll be there soon."

She nodded, not bothering to look his way. Or maybe she didn't have the energy. "We'd be there a lot sooner if I could move a little faster."

"Don't push yourself. You'll end up on the ground again."

"I won't. I'd rather not repeat the experience."

"Me, neither. I lost ten years of my life the last time. I can't afford to lose any more."

As he'd hoped, the comment caught her attention and this time she did look his way, a grin lighting her face and easing some of the pain and tension there. "I scared you, huh?"

"*Scared* isn't a strong enough word. Look close. You'll probably see a streak of white in my hair."

"If there is, I'll buy you a box of hair color when we get home."

"How about a steak dinner instead?"

"Steak or seafood. Your choice."

"Both."

"It's a deal." She smiled again and Noah linked his arm through hers, pulling her a little closer, listening to the wheezing gasp of her breath, and praying that she'd be around to make good on her part of the bargain.

The change was subtle at first—the trees not quite so tightly packed together, the ground not as thick with foliage, jungle dimness replaced by brighter sunlight. Soon deep jungle gave way to sporadic trees and Tori almost groaned with relief when Noah led her into what must have once been a village. Piles of debris littered the ground, evidence of a community that had left long ago. One hut remained standing. Solitary, broken, it stood in the middle of the clearing, vines and ivy trailing up the stilt-legs and bamboo sides. The door was a black hole. The windows were dark and empty. The stairs that would have given the owners access were gone, the space beneath the hut shadowed. *Creepy* was the word Tori would have used to describe it if she'd had the breath to speak. She didn't, so she just collapsed onto the ground, resting her cheek against her knees, and watching as Simon stepped into view. He wasn't alone. Hawke strolled behind him, his scar a deep purple slash down the side of his face, his gaze on Tori, watchful, alert and just short of concerned. "Looks like you made it after all."

She nodded, but didn't have the breath to respond.

Hawke turned his attention to Noah. "I guess you have a plan for getting her back?"

"Helicopter."

"And risk letting Lao know we're here?"

"We'll wait until we check the village. If we don't get Melody out before the chopper arrives she's as good as dead."

"And if the girl isn't there?"

"Then Simon will take Tori back to the safe house and you and I will keep looking."

Hawke's lip curled, his eyes cold as he turned his attention to Tori again. "You'd better start praying to that God of yours, Stone. 'Cause I can tell you right now, your lady friend isn't gonna make it back to Mae Hong Son under her own power."

"I'll make it." Tori lifted her head, ignoring the pounding pain behind her eyes and the way the world dipped and spun around her.

"So there's still some life in you." He crouched down in front of her, his eyes scanning her face.

"There's plenty of life left in me." She gritted her teeth and started to rise, but Hawke laid a hand on her arm and held her down.

"Now's not the time to prove it. Here. Something for the pain." He pulled two white tablets from his pack and handed them to her.

"What are they?"

He grinned. "Afraid I'm passing you something illegal?"

"Just want to make sure it's nothing I'm allergic to."

"You're not allergic to anything, are you, Doc?"

"Doc?"

"Heard you were a vet."

"I am."

"Then you'll know that Tylenol 3 isn't going to hurt you. Just take one for now. Save the other for later. If you end up walking back, you'll need it."

She took the tablets, her face heating at what she'd assumed. "Thank you."

"Water?" Noah handed her a bottle and Tori gulped down the first tablet.

But it was Hawke who stayed crouched beside her, watching with solemn eyes. "Give it a few minutes. You'll be feeling better."

"I guess I can't feel much worse."

"That's the spirit." He stood, nodded toward Noah. "Time for business. You going into the village, Stone?"

"Just close enough to see if I can spot Lao's men."

"Simon, you're his backup. I'll stay with the lady."

"That would be a waste of manpower. I'll be fine here on my own." What Tori's voice lacked in strength it made up for in conviction.

Noah turned toward her, ready to argue, but Hawke saved him the effort.

"I don't recall asking your opinion."

"I'm giving it anyway. I don't need a babysitter."

"Think of me as your bodyguard."

"I don't need a bodyguard, either."

"You might. This isn't a place to be out on your

own." Noah forced a calm into his voice that he didn't feel and knelt by Tori, scanning her face, trying to determine how bad off she was.

He didn't like what he was seeing. Pale skin still flushed with what he now suspected was fever, her eyes glassy and bright in a face pinched with anxiety, she looked ill. Too ill to walk back to Mae Hong Son. No matter how slow the pace.

He was surprised when her hot, dry fingers linked through his.

When she spoke, her words were soft, meant for him and not the other men that stood just feet away. "Stop worrying."

"I thought that was my line."

"Not this time." She squeezed his hand, let hers fall away. "Go find Melody. That's what matters right now."

"Not all that matters. Hang in there, Red. I won't be any longer than I need to be." He started to rise, but Tori grabbed his hand again.

"You're right. Melody isn't all that matters. Be careful, Noah."

Something in his chest tightened at her words, at her acknowledgment of the bond that had been growing between them since the moment he'd walked into the room in Chiang Mai and seen her chained to the wall and still fighting. "I will be. Just make sure you're here when I come back."

"Where would I go?"

"Whichever direction you think Melody might be."

"Not this time."

"Good. I'm counting on it." He ran his knuckles along her jaw, then rose, turning toward Simon. "Let's go see what we can find out."

Tori watched Noah disappear into the jungle, the feel of his fingers still warm on her jaw.

"Good man, that." Hawke leaned against a tree, studying Tori.

"He seems to be, but people aren't always what they seem."

"Sometimes the surface hides the truth. Sometimes it is the truth."

"Meaning?"

"Noah Stone is what you see. Nothing hidden. Nothing dark. Not like you and me."

"Dark and hidden? I think I'm insulted." She tried to make light of his words, but Hawke didn't smile, didn't shift his gaze from hers.

"Are you? Why? You know that I am saying nothing but the truth."

"No. I don't." But the sinking feeling in her gut said she did, that everything that had happened in the past had marked her, darkened her soul just as Hawke had claimed.

"I see you're reconsidering your position."

"I'm not in the mood for games, Hawke. Say what you need to and get it over with."

"Good enough. Noah Stone is one of the few people I trust with my life. I want happiness for him."

"What does that have to do with me?"

"That you ask proves my point. Noah would have the guts to say what he felt, not hide behind questions."

"Now I really am insulted."

He grinned, but there was no humor in his eyes. "Just so we understand each other."

"Yeah, we understand each other. You don't like me, and I don't like you."

Hawke's laughter was harsh and rusty. "Maybe you'll do after all, Victoria Riley."

"I don't—"

Hawke held up a hand and motioned her to silence, all expression gone from his face, his eyes hard, cold steel.

Tori froze, not daring to move, barely daring to breathe. She heard nothing, but Hawke grabbed her hand and yanked her into the thick foliage at the edge of the clearing. One minute she was on her feet, the next she was lying on the ground, Hawke's hand on her shoulder holding her down.

He bent close, whispering into her ear. "Don't move."

Then he left so silently Tori wouldn't have known he'd gone if she hadn't been watching him. Minutes ticked by, the rustle of grass and soft sigh of leaves the only sounds Tori heard. The urge to get up and look around taunted her, but Hawke's expression had been too grim and hard for her to chance moving before he returned. Obviously, he'd sensed danger, but from where?

She peered toward the hut, but the plant cover was too dense for her to see much beyond the place where she lay. Maybe that was a good thing. If she couldn't see the danger, she could pretend she was safe.

No, that wasn't her style. Tori liked knowing what lurked in the shadows. Only then could she defend herself against it. At least that's how she'd felt before coming to Thailand. Now she thought she might be content to lie here for days, waiting for Noah, Hawke and Simon to take care of whoever might be waiting to pounce.

She closed her eyes, trying to come up with a plan, but her mind was blank, her thoughts so jumbled there wasn't one clear idea to build on. The only thing she knew for sure was that she was alone. She could feel it as surely as she could feel the scrape of dry leaves beneath her arms and the dull throb of pain in her side.

More time passed. Nothing moved. No snap of twigs or pad of feet on the ground to tell her Hawke was returning. Shouldn't he be back by now? Had he been hurt? Killed? She shifted to her knees, but couldn't quite get up the nerve to stand and look around.

"This is ridiculous." She muttered the words to herself as she dropped back down and pressed her cheek to the ground.

"Good choice." Noah spoke quietly from somewhere behind her and Tori jumped, barely biting back a scream.

Chapter Sixteen

"Do you always have to sneak up on me?"

"I wasn't sneaking. Just being quiet enough not to attract attention." His voice was flat, his mouth a tight line of pain or anger. Tori wasn't sure which.

She pushed herself up and was on her feet so fast she felt dizzy, all thoughts of Hawke and danger gone in her rush to hear news about Melody. "Did you find her? Is she there?"

"Lao's men are there. Looks like they're guarding one of the huts."

"Then Melody must be in it."

"That's a good possibility, but we can't know for sure until we get inside. Simon's still there. If he can, he'll get a look inside the hut."

"And if he can't?"

"We'll wait until tonight, create a distraction and access the hut then."

"And waste hours? You said yourself that our time was limited. Maybe we should search some of the other villages while we're waiting."

"*We're* not searching anywhere."

"Fine. Maybe *you* should search some of the other villages while we're waiting."

"I could, but my gut says Melody's here."

"I don't have much faith in gut instinct."

"Red, you don't have much faith in anything." There was no bite to the words, but Tori felt the need to defend herself.

"I have faith in myself. That's enough."

"Is it?"

The answer should have been easy, but it wasn't. She raised a shaky hand and rubbed at the tension in her neck. "It used to be. Now I'm not so sure."

"Then you're halfway there. Come on. Hawke's figured out a way into the hut."

"You mean I've been lying in the dirt so he could figure out how to get into that shack? I thought we'd been discovered."

"You were." A clipped, stark answer that left Tori feeling sick.

"What happened?"

"Hawke did what he had to do to protect the mission."

"He killed someone?" She knew she sounded horrified. She felt horrified. "That can't be. I've been right here. I didn't hear or see a thing."

"You weren't meant to. Come on. We'll stay in the hut until sundown." Lines of fatigue fanned out around his eyes, and tension radiated from him in waves.

He looked weary, and for the first time since their ordeal began, Tori wondered what it had cost him to come back to the place where he'd almost died. "I'm sorry you've been dragged into this, Noah."

"Don't be. It wasn't your choice for me to come."

"I know, but—"

"We'll talk it all out, but not now." He moved away before she could say more and she had no choice but to follow.

Hawke stood beside the hut, his gaze hooded as he watched their approach. There was a mark on his cheek that hadn't been there before, a small nick above his scar that bled just enough to send a trickle of red down his face. Other than that, he looked the same, unmoved by the battle he'd just fought or the life he'd taken.

He'd said there was darkness inside him. Tori believed it. Though she'd seen something else, as well—loyalty, maybe even compassion.

Noah strode forward and tugged on a rope that was wrapped around the top edge of the bamboo wall. "Think it'll hold one of us?"

"We'll find out in a minute." Hawke pulled himself up. Within seconds his hands were on the top section of the wall. He heaved himself up and disappeared from sight.

"We'll meet him around the other side."

Tori didn't think it mattered what side they were on. No way would she be able to make it up the rope, let alone pull herself over the wall. "I'm not so sure this is a good idea."

"Going into the hut?"

"Me trying to climb the rope."

"You won't have to. Hawke's going to pull you up."

"That's an even worse idea."

"Afraid he'll drop you?"

"No. I'm afraid he'll break his back."

"You worry too much, you know that?"

Tori shrugged, her gaze on the doorway as Hawke appeared, the rope dangling from one hand.

He tossed it down. "Loop it under her arms, Stone."

It took only seconds for Hawke to pull her through the door opening. Tori tumbled into the dingy room, her feet dragging through layers of dirt, leaves and other things she'd rather not name.

Noah followed seconds later, his dark hair falling across his forehead. "Looks like the place has been empty for years, unless you count rats and mice."

He took off his pack, pulled out a blanket and Tori's poncho, spread the first on the floor and handed her the second. "Go ahead and get comfortable. We'll be here for a while."

"What about you and Hawke?"

"We've both slept on worse than this before." Noah stretched out a few feet away, his pack under his head, his eyes closing almost immediately.

Hawke did the same, lying down near the window and using his pack as a pillow. Neither spoke again. Were they asleep? It didn't seem possible. Not with the threat of danger lurking beyond the hut's flimsy walls. Yet neither moved and both seemed completely relaxed. Maybe Tori should take her cue from them.

She tried, easing down onto the blanket and closing her eyes, but her mind was humming with questions and worries.

She turned onto her side so that she faced Noah and Hawke. "Do you think Simon will be back soon?"

Hawke didn't respond, but Noah opened his eyes and met Tori's gaze. "Depends on how long it takes him to get a look in the hut."

"And he's coming here once he knows for sure that Melody's there?"

"Right."

"So how's he going to find us if we're all up here?"

"He'll find us."

"How? Hawke's already pulled in the rope. What if Simon—"

"He'll signal. Hawke will drop the rope and Simon will climb up. Simple."

"But if we're asleep—"

"We'll hear him."

"But—"

"We'll hear him. Now stop worrying and close your eyes."

"I can't. Every time I close them I see Melody all alone and afraid."

"She's not alone. She knows that you and her parents won't rest until she's home. And she's got God. He hasn't abandoned her."

"I wish I could believe that."

"You don't have to. Melody does. That will see her through."

That was true. Melody's faith was as deep as her parents'. "She's just so young."

"Not much younger than you were when you had her."

"Maybe not in years, but in every other way."

"Young but strong. Like her mother."

"Joi's been a great example for her."

"That may be true, but I was talking about you."

"I'm not her mother." After all this time, it shouldn't hurt to say it, but there was still a part of Tori that mourned what she couldn't have.

"Not in the truest sense of the word, but you gave birth to her, you gave her wonderful parents. You also gave her red hair, freckles, a slim build. Those things are in her genetic code. Just like being a survivor is. Now close your eyes and try to rest. We've got a long night ahead of us." The words were a gentle dismissal. Noah's closed eyes reinforced the point.

Sunlight streamed into the hut, the walls offering little shade. Tori's clothes stuck to her skin and her throat felt parched, but she didn't want to disturb Noah again. Instead she lay still and silent, imagining herself at home, lying on the porch swing, a tall glass of lemonade beside her.

Would she ever get back to Lakeview?

Right now, home seemed a faraway dream. A place whose uncomplicated rhythm was more imagination than reality, the predictable, never-ending routine of it more blessing than curse. After years of wanting to get away, Tori wanted to go home.

She closed her eyes, a prayer hovering in her mind, but Hawke's words mocked her, stilling the words before they could form.

He'd been right.

There *was* darkness inside of her. Years of living life on her own terms, of ignoring the quiet voice inside that begged her to revisit the faith she'd had as a child, had left her empty and stained with guilt. For the first time in years, Tori wished she hadn't turned away from God when her father died. But she had, and now all she could do was hope that He cared enough about Melody and the Raymonds to intervene on their behalf.

She sighed, twisting position, the heat of the day

and her own fatigue conspiring to do what Tori had thought impossible, relaxing her tense muscles and stealing her anxiety until her worries disappeared into sleep, her last conscious thought that perhaps Melody and the Raymonds weren't the only ones God would intervene for. Perhaps, despite her sins, He loved Tori enough to intervene for her, as well.

It was full dark when she woke, heart slamming against her ribs, pain knifing through her side. For a moment she didn't know where she was, and imagined herself back in Lakeview. Then the hardness of her bed and the musty scent of age and neglect stirred her memory. Mae Hong Son. The jungle. The rotting hut in the middle of the overgrown clearing.

Tori sat up, trying to see through the thick blanket of night, but all she could see was darkness.

"Noah?" She whispered his name. "Hawke?"

Neither answered, and Tori crawled across the floor, heading in the direction of the door. The waning moon had yet to crest the rise of trees and mountains, and the area below the hut was painted in shades of black. If someone was there, Tori couldn't see him.

Leaves rustled in the thick trees that surrounded the clearing—a predator or its prey moving through the night. Tori stood still, forcing herself to a calm she didn't feel. There wasn't a glimmer of light, no evidence of the village Simon had gone to explore. Where was he? Where were Noah and Hawke?

She wanted to call out, but was afraid her words would carry on the mountain air. Instead, she leaned out the doorway, searching the shadows, trying to find evidence that one of the men was below.

"Better be careful, that bamboo isn't sturdy." Noah's voice broke the silence, so unexpected, Tori nearly toppled from her perch.

"I was wondering where you were."

"Close by." He stepped out of the thick shadows that lined the edge of the clearing. "Simon's back. Melody is in the hut."

Tori's heart leapt with the news. "He's sure?"

"He saw her. But we're only halfway to the goal. We still need to get her out."

"When?"

"Soon. Come on, I'll help you down."

She lowered herself to the floor and shimmied over the edge of the doorway. Her body ached, her hands swollen and clumsy as she tried to get a grip on the edge of the doorway. The old wood felt slick beneath her palms, and before she could get a firm hold she was falling.

She landed in Noah's arms with a thud, and lay stunned against his chest.

"That was close." His voice rumbled in her ear and shivered along her spine.

"Thanks for catching me."

"Did you think I'd let you fall?"

"Other people have." The words slipped out, and she wished she could take them back.

"Not me." He pulled her a bit closer, then slowly lowered her to the ground.

She wasn't sure how to respond, didn't know if she should respond at all, so she took a step away, raked a hand through tangled hair. "Where are Simon and Hawke?"

"Checking things out at the village. Once they get back we'll implement our plan."

"If you've got a plan, why not implement it now?"

"We need to find out what Lao's men are up to. Get a feel for how many are guarding the hut Melody is in. A recovery like this takes time."

"How much time?"

"Enough to be sure we do it right."

She swallowed back the protest that danced on the tip of her tongue. "Are you going to tell me what the plan is?"

"Let's wait until they get back. Plans might change depending on what they find."

"But—"

He cut her off, leaning close so she could see his eyes gleaming in the darkness. "Here's what you do need to know before they return. Simon, Hawke and I have worked together before. We know what we're doing. We've planned and coordinated our moves to the second. You've got one job to do. Stay where we leave you. Don't move. Don't run. Don't try to rush to the rescue."

"I understand."

"Do you?"

"I know what's at risk, Noah. Your life. Hawke's. Simon's. Melody's. I won't take any chances."

"That's what you're saying now, but you're a maverick, not a team player. When push comes to shove and things don't go the way you think they should, you'll be tempted to step in and help out. You do and we'll all be in trouble."

He was right. She'd spent too many years depending on herself to find depending on others easy. But this time she didn't have a choice. "Like I said, I won't take chances."

"Good." His fingers skimmed along her jaw. "Did a few hours' sleep do you any good?"

"Sure."

"That doesn't sound too convincing."

"I'm all right. I'm more worried about Melody. Did she look okay? Could Simon see if she'd been hurt?"

"He only caught a glimpse. The good news is that none of Lao's men entered the hut. The only person who came or went was an old lady. Simon thinks she's the medicine woman. He heard some talk about curses and God. Thinks maybe the old woman is protecting Melody by telling Lao's men they've angered the Christian God and will bring a curse down on themselves and their families if they harm her. They may be just superstitious enough to believe it."

"You two ready?" Simon's voice slid into the darkness seconds before his shadowy figure appeared beside Noah. "Looks like Lao's men are drinking themselves into a stupor. Now's as good a time as any to move."

"We're ready. Where's your brother?"

"Here. Just not much in the mood for conversation." Hawke's voice was gritty and hard, but Tori was still glad to hear it. She might not know much about rescue missions, but it seemed three people working together had better odds of success than two.

Maybe.

"How many of Lao's men are in the village?" Tori directed the question toward anyone willing to answer.

Noah was in front of her, a blacker darkness against the jungle. She thought she heard him sigh. "A few."

"How many is a few? Three? Four? Twenty?"

"Twelve." Hawke's whisper was ripe with irritation. "Thirteen if you count Lao. I don't. He's worthless as a fighter. Now shut up before they hear us and come looking."

Tori ignored him, keeping her voice low. "Thirteen of them and three of you? I don't like the odds."

"We don't need to worry about the odds. Not with what we've got planned." Noah's words were barely a rumble in the darkness.

"Maybe you can explain the plan before we head out."

Someone yanked her arm, pulling her around.

"You want to know the plans?" Hawke whispered close to her ear, and she nodded, forcing back the fear that shivered up her spine.

"I'm part of this. I should know what you're going to do."

"Then listen up and when I'm done talking, so are you. Got it?"

"I'll be done talking when—"

Noah's whisper cut through the darkness. "We don't have time to argue. Explain what we've got planned and let's move out."

Hawke muttered something. Maybe a curse. Maybe a protest. Then he spoke, his whisper razor sharp. "Simon and I will play ghost, haunt the perimeter of the village, make enough noise to spook Lao's men and draw them away from their posts. Once we've got them on the move, Noah's going in. He'll free the girl and get her out of the village."

It sounded so easy, so simple. But it wasn't, and the night was heavy with the knowledge of just how difficult things might get. Tori could almost feel adrenaline pulsing through the air. She imagined the three men stalking through the darkness, easing through the shadows. Could see them fighting, dying. And the sour taste of bile rose in her throat. "Maybe you should wait for backup. Surely someone's close enough—"

"I've already called for a helicopter. We've got to have Melody out before it gets close."

Noah didn't need to explain why. Tori took a deep, shuddering breath, forcing back more questions. Telling herself she had to do what was best for Melody and hardest for herself—trust someone else to do a job she wanted and needed to do herself. "Then what are we waiting for?"

She wasn't sure, but she thought Noah chuckled, the sound so quiet, it barely stirred the air.

Chapter Seventeen

The men moved like wraiths, so silent Tori would have lost her way if not for Noah's tight grip on her hand. The only branches that broke were under Tori's feet, the only harsh, gasping breaths, her own. She knew it would have been better for everyone if she'd stayed with Joi and Mark. If, like Melody's parents, she'd had the ability to trust in others. And to trust in God.

The thought wouldn't leave her alone as she trudged through dense jungle, the hiss of night creatures alive around her. She'd spent most of her life working things out on her own, finding solutions—sometimes not the best—for her problems. Maybe if she'd once looked beyond her own knowledge, her own steady belief that she was on her own, she might have found God waiting patiently for her to turn and ask directions.

Regret was like a stone in her belly, the weight dragging down her already-weary spirit. Sweat beaded her brow, heat radiating from the swollen flesh of her wrists. She could almost feel the bacteria marching through her bloodstream, poisoning her body. Worse, though, was the way her doubt had poisoned the efforts to find Melody. Slowing Noah down, keeping him from doing what he did best.

"This is it." The words were a gentle touch against her cheek, barely there, but shivering along Tori's nerves. Noah's hand cupped her jaw, turning her head until she could see tiny lights shimmering in the distance. No bigger than fireflies, they winked and waved. Candlelight?

Tori didn't ask. Didn't even speak for fear her voice would carry through the darkness. Instead, she nodded against Noah's hand.

"That's where we're headed. You'll stay here. Simon, Hawke and I paced this spot out. We'll have no trouble finding you when we're finished. Unless you move."

"I won't." The words caught in her throat, the urge to apologize again, to beg him to be careful, not just for Melody's sake, but for his own, burning on her tongue.

Noah tried to believe her as he pulled Tori to a clump of ferns. Wide fronds would protect her from sight if she stayed down—and that was something Tori didn't seem to be good at.

Noah kept his doubts and worries to himself. Just urged her down onto the jungle floor. "Scoot under the ferns. Use their leaves as cover."

He could hear her wiggling her way into the foliage, imagined her pale skin flecked with dirt and white with fear. She was more vulnerable than any of them, her lack of skills making her survival doubtful if something should happen to Noah and the men who accompanied him.

But he couldn't think on that now. Not when so much

depended on his complete focus. Hawke and Simon hovered nearby, impatient to move, though neither spoke.

Noah waited until the rustle of leaves and slide of fabric faded to silence. Then he stepped back from the spot where Tori hid, looking for a shimmer of white, any sign that she was there. When he found none, he turned to face the dark shadows that were Hawke and Simon. "Give me ten. Then start the game."

He moved quickly, jogging along a path that was little more than a dirt ribbon through the wilderness, moving by memory and instinct rather than by sight. If things worked out, Lao's men would be too drunk to use reason and smarts when Hawke and Simon began their part of the mission. He prayed Lao would send them out anyway. With surprise on his side, Noah figured he could overpower anyone left behind to guard Melody. If not, he'd be dodging bullets and running for cover. Nothing he hadn't done before, but something he'd sworn he'd never do again—slinking through a jungle alive with predators and heavy with the scent of life and death, hope and desperation.

Why? It was a question he'd been asking himself since he'd taken this assignment. One he was only now beginning to find answers for. He was here for Melody, to save her and bring her home. He was here to secure the box and the information it contained. But he was here for another reason, as well. Tori. Not just to assure her safety, but to help her rebuild her trust in others.

And maybe something more.

But that thought, like so many others, was best left for another time.

He was close to the village now. So close he could

hear laughter and voices, see the dark shapes of huts and people. A few hundred yards in diameter, twenty huts, chickens, goats and a few dogs. He'd seen it all earlier, memorized the location of the hut where Melody was being kept. He skirted the perimeter, a clock ticking in his head, counting off minutes and the time he had left to make it into position.

There was the ravine—steep, treacherous—but he'd moved through it earlier in the day and was at the bottom in minutes, slogging across wet ground and moving up the other side. Creeping closer to the village, using brush and trees to hide himself, moving so silently the night creatures never gave up their songs.

Lanterns burned in the windows of the huts, open windows covered by sheer fabric or by nothing at all. The hut Noah sought stood at the edge of the village.

A miscalculation Lao and his men would pay for.

Nothing moved inside, a lone light shining from within the only indication that it was occupied. Like the other huts in the village, this one was on stilts, a fenced area beneath providing ample space for a garden or livestock. Two men paced near the stairs that led to the hut's door. One of them lit a cigarette, the flash of fire and burning embers making him an easy target.

Noah inched closer.

Time! The word shouted through his mind and Noah didn't need to look at his watch to know it was true. He checked anyway, dropping down into a crouch, hiding himself in the shadows and smiling grimly as somewhere at the far edge of the village a man shouted a warning.

Hawke and Simon had begun.

Noah stayed hunkered down, waiting for confusion

to draw Lao's men out, watching the guards, hoping they might move off, too. He was prepared to do what he had to if they didn't.

And while Noah waited he prayed, not for his own safety, but for the safety of the men who were risking everything for a girl they didn't know, for a cause they probably didn't believe in. Men who knew nothing of God and for whom death would be a final, painful blow.

Tori shifted, her stomach knotted with tension, her muscles screaming for movement and action. Dampness seeped into her clothes and wormed its way into her bones. She shivered uncontrollably, gritting her teeth to keep them from chattering. For several minutes she'd been hearing voices, distant shouts, the words muted. Now there was a cacophony of noise, the sounds reverberating through the night and striking against Tori's eardrums and her nerves.

Despite the coolness of the mountain air, the night felt cloying, smothering her beneath its weight. The moist, musty scent of the forest reminded her of fall days when she was young—of tent revivals and snapping bonfires, of songs and praise, worship and prayer. She'd felt like an outsider there, surrounded by the fervent and fevered, her stepfather leading them all in singing and shouted Psalms, his hot eyes boring into Tori's, demanding she participate. And she had, the words sour on her tongue, her heart hard as stone.

Here, though, she felt what she'd never felt on those cool, crisp nights. A stirring of her spirit. The strange and not altogether comfortable feeling that she was not alone. That faith hovered just out of reach, God's whisper to her soul, His silent voice calling to her.

She shuddered, trying to shake the feeling, telling herself that she was imagining things.

But she wasn't. She knew it, just as she knew she'd never been alone. Not through the darkness of her father's illness and death. Not during the years she'd lived under her stepfather's iron control. Not when she'd turned her back on God and everything He offered.

Not now.

She didn't doubt the knowledge. She only wondered what she'd do with it.

She shifted again, uneasy in the sudden hush of the jungle. In the distance, men still shouted, but closer to Tori, the night creatures had silenced, their rustling movements and calls gone. She strained to hear above the erratic thump of her own terror. Was that a branch breaking? The soft tread of someone approaching?

Then it happened. A shout much closer than the others. A shrill cry. A smattering of cracks and pops that sounded like firecrackers, but were probably gunfire. Tori jerked up, then remembered Noah's warning and her own assurance that she'd stay where he'd left her. She sank back down, burrowing farther into the ferns.

Another shout followed the first. This one so close, Tori was sure she could reach out and touch the speaker. Garbled words spewed into the blackness, then faded as prey and pursuer fled into the night. Tori sank deeper into her cover, knowing more men might follow. Leaves tickled against her cheek and neck. A stone dug into the tender flesh on her stomach. And still she waited.

She grimaced, shifted, felt something move to her right, heard the rustle and crackle of leaves beneath feet. She tensed, wanting to run, knowing she couldn't. Then a hand was in her hair, fisted tight and yanking her up. She didn't scream. There wasn't time. One minute she was lying on the ground. The next she was up, a man's arm around her waist. His hand across her mouth.

"I thought I'd find you somewhere nearby. Where's the box? Give it to me now and I might not kill you. Then again, maybe I will, just for all the trouble you've caused me."

Tori knew the voice, the heavily accented English, the dark laughter that slid like silk along her nerves, only barely covering the death that lurked behind it. He'd visited her many times when she'd been imprisoned, had seemed to be the leader of the group that had abducted Tori.

Lao. It had to be.

She struggled against his hold, knowing his strength and his cruelty, wondering where Simon and Hawke were. Where Noah was. Did they have Melody? Was she safe? Were they?

The questions flashed through her mind as Lao dragged her a few steps back. She twisted, looked up into his face, could barely make out the broad, flat face or the strange goggles he wore. Night-vision goggles? Did all his men have them? Or only Lao? The thought of Simon and Hawke trying to escape an army of better-equipped men filled Tori with cold dread. Would they all die here in the jungle, their bodies left for the scavengers to find? Had they been brought this far to fail?

No. She wouldn't believe that. No matter her doubts, she had to believe there was hope, that somehow they'd survive.

"Well? Will you give it to me this time? Or do we

have to continue where we left off?" His fingers dug into Tori's ribs as he spoke, emphasizing the point.

Do something! Do it now! The thoughts shouted through Tori's mind and she obeyed, slamming the heel of her foot into Lao's knee, then reaching for his face, tearing at the night-vision goggles he wore, ripping them off. Something cracked and Lao cursed, his grip loosening. She twisted hard, shoving her elbow into his gut and jerking away.

Which way? She didn't know if she should move toward the village or away. Was afraid she'd somehow lead Lao to Melody and Noah. She dodged behind a tree, crouching low and sprinting forward. Not sure where she was heading, not knowing if Lao was following, barely able to see in the darkness.

Still she ran, tripping, skidding in moist earth, then tumbling down a steep ravine, every bone in her body jarred.

She clambered to her feet and would have raced forward again, but a hard arm slid around her waist, jerking her backward.

"I thought you said you'd stay put." The words were hissed in her ear, the anger behind them obvious, but the voice was one she recognized, one she'd been longing to hear.

"Noah! He's here. Lao is here. He had night-vision goggles. What if the other men have them, too? Hawke and Simon—"

"Slow down. Take it easy. Tell me what's going on." Noah's grip tightened, though his voice smoothed, a calm facade for the storm Tori suspected was brewing.

"Lao. He found me. I don't know how. I did what I promised, but he was there anyway. What are we going to do? What about Melody?" Her teeth were chattering so hard, she could barely speak, her hands clutching at Noah's arms, fear that he would go off in search of Lao and leave her alone again making her want to cling.

"Shhh." He smoothed a hand down her back, his lips brushing against her ear, then her cheek, as he pressed her closer to his chest. "She's fine. I've got her."

"Where?"

"Come on out." The words were barely above a whisper, but leaves rustled nearby.

Tori turned toward the sound, saw a figure ease from the foliage. If the sun were shining through the trees, Tori knew it would glint on deep red hair.

Melody. Alive. Safe.

Tori stepped toward her, relief loosening muscles held tense for too long. She opened her mouth, would have spoken, but Noah moved so quickly, so suddenly, she didn't realize what was happening until his hand was over her mouth, his lips pressed close to her ear. "Listen."

She froze, heard crashing branches and heavy footfalls.

"Lao's coming, and he's not being quiet about it. Which means he doesn't know I'm here, yet." He turned her so she was facing him, bent so close she could see the gleam of his eyes in the darkness. "You trust me?"

There was no time to think about it, no time to second-guess herself. She could hear Lao crashing through the trees, knew he'd be there in seconds. "Yes."

"Then lie on the ground, like you've fallen. Close your eyes. Play dead."

Play dead? Another plan with a million holes, but this time Tori didn't bother to think of any of them. Noah had gotten her this far and she'd have to have faith he'd bring her the rest of the way home. Faith. Something she hadn't known she could possess. Something she'd been afraid to trust. Now she had no choice.

She lowered herself to the ground and lay without moving while the sound of breaking branches and crushed leaves drew closer.

Chapter Eighteen

The jungle was alive with the sounds of gunfire and pursuit, but Tori lay still as death, not moving as dirt and leaves peppered the ground near her head and something large and heavy landed with a thud by her feet.

It was Lao. She could smell the sickly sweet fragrance of his cologne and had to fight the urge to gag. She felt his breath on her face as he ran a hand over her hair. The urge to slam her fist into his stomach was almost overwhelming, but Noah's question raced through her mind.

Do you trust me?

Could she?

If she couldn't, now was the time for action. But she lay still as Lao grabbed a handful of her hair and yanked. Something cold and hard pressed against her scalp, but she didn't open her eyes.

Play dead. For Melody. For Noah.

A lock of hair fell against her cheek, and she knew what Lao was doing. Cutting her hair.

Or was he going to scalp her?

She braced herself for the cold, sharp edge of steel cutting into her skin. Instead there was a whoosh of sound, a grunt, a thud, and she was being pulled to her feet, Noah's voice speaking words she couldn't quite understand. "Are you okay? Tori! Did he cut you?"

"No. I'm okay. Where's Melody?"

"Right here." Melody's voice trembled out, the sound so welcome Tori's eyes filled with tears.

She grabbed the teen, hugging her close. "Are you okay? Did they hurt you?"

"I'm fine."

Noah's hand landed on Tori's shoulder. "We can talk more later. Right now we need to get out of here before Lao comes to."

"You didn't kill him?"

"Would you rather I had?"

"No."

"Good. We'll let the police take care of him. No more talking. The rest of Lao's men are still on the hunt."

They moved quickly, silently, Noah leading, his hand firm and strong around Tori's. Melody clung to Tori's other hand, her grip tighter and more desperate, as if she were afraid to let go, afraid her safety would slip away and she'd be lost forever.

Tori knew the feeling only too well. Her own anxiety nipped at her heels as she moved through the deep jungle. If she'd been the one leading she would have run, racing down the mountain and away from danger. Already the world was lightening, the shadows of night easing into gray. Soon there would be nothing between them and discovery but trees. She grimaced at the thought, wishing she could push Noah to move faster, knowing he wouldn't—for her sake if nothing else.

She wanted to tell him she was okay, that numbness had replaced pain, but she was afraid to speak, afraid any sound might bring danger back toward them.

Somewhere nearby a branch snapped. Leaves rustled, and Tori was sure she could hear the soft sigh of someone's breath drifting on the predawn air. Noah either didn't notice or wasn't worried by the sound. He kept the same, slow, steady pace, never faltering, never hesitating.

She didn't know where he was leading, only knew that he had a destination. Some predetermined meeting place, perhaps. It didn't take long to reach it—a village, gray in the early-morning gloom. Smaller than the village where Tori had met Doom, this one had only ten huts arranged in a semicircle in the middle of a large clearing. There were no animals, no chickens, nothing moving. The place looked abandoned, though some instinct warned that it was not.

"Where are we?" Tori dared the whisper, her throat so dry she could barely force the words out.

"Another one of Lao's strongholds. It's an easier place for the chopper to land than the last village." Noah stopped them a hundred yards out, keeping them in a grove of thick trees, hiding them in the early-morning shadows. Mist danced across the ground, swirling around Tori's legs, kissing the sides of the stilt-legged huts and shrouding gated yards.

Nothing moved. No one stirred. The hush seemed both eerie and unnatural.

"I don't like the way this feels. Our men are supposed to be here already. Seems they haven't made it."

"What are we going to do?" Tori hoped she didn't sound as scared as she felt.

"The helicopter can't be far. Hawke and Simon are supposed to rendezvous here, too."

"So we wait?"

"You and Melody wait. I'm going in to see how many of Lao's men are there."

"What? Why?"

"Because I can't let the chopper fly into a trap. The deal was we'd have this place cleared out before it arrived. Something's gone wrong. I need to correct it."

"Alone?"

"I'm never alone." He pulled his gun, his face grim in the waxing light. "You and Melody stay here.'

Melody's grip tightened on Tori's hand as Noah slipped from the cover of the trees. Perhaps she wondered what would happen if he didn't return. In her mind Noah must be a hero, a man who'd appeared out of nowhere, saved her from a terrifying ordeal and promised to take her home.

And maybe he was a hero.

Tori had always thought heroes were the stuff of fiction, but now, as she watched Noah disappear into the jungle, she knew she'd been wrong.

She wanted to call him back, tell him what she was thinking, let him know how much she appreciated all that he'd done.

Instead, she choked back her own fear and squeezed Melody's hand. "It'll be okay."

The words were barely out when the crack of gunfire split the air. There was a crash, a curse, the sound of a struggle. Tori jumped, yanking Melody down to the ground and throwing herself on top of her. Her own body would be a poor shield against a bullet, but it was all Tori had.

"Come out, and your friend lives. Make us search for you and he dies." The words were thick and hard, the English more refined than Lao's.

Tori's mind scrambled for a plan. Did they really have Noah? Or were they bluffing? Could she afford to wait and find out?

"You have five minutes. Then we shoot him."

Sweat trickled down her brow, the weight of the choice she had to make lead against her chest.

"Tori. Tori, did you hear me?"

Melody's voice shook with fright, and Tori forced herself to focus on the words, to look into her daughter's wide, fear-filled eyes. "Sorry. What?"

"We need to pray. We need to ask for help."

"Sweetie..." But what could she say? That everything Melody believed was a lie? That the only answers they'd get were ones of their own making?

Or were they?

If there was nothing to be counted on but her own resources, what had Tori experienced in those moments before Lao grabbed her? Could she shrug off the feeling she'd had that she wasn't alone, that the God she'd turned away from had never turned from her? Could she pretend what she'd felt had been nothing but her imagination? Pretend it hadn't happened?

And if she did, would she ever again have the chance to grasp what she'd always wanted—faith in something beyond herself and her own ability.

She pushed aside her doubt, tried to smile at Melody. "You're right. I should have thought of that myself."

The prayer was rusty, the words awkward, but the feeling was there, the desperation and the hope that the prayer was heard.

When she finished she knew what she had to do.

"Listen to me, Melody. Noah's not coming back. Something's happened. I've got to go find him. I want you to stay here. If I don't come back—"

"No. Don't leave me here!" Melody's panic was real, her hands grasping Tori's shirt, pulling her close.

"I have to. You're strong and brave. The best kid I know. Stay here. Don't move. Cover yourself with dirt and leaves and *don't move.* No matter what. A helicopter will be here soon."

"I can't stay here alone."

"You won't be alone. God's with you." She kissed Melody on the cheek, eased from her grip. "Do what I said."

"I will." Tears streaked down Melody's face, mixing with the dirt there. "I love you, Tori."

"I love you, too."

Then Tori was moving, sliding on her belly, away from Melody and the safety of the jungle. She didn't move straight into the open, but eased through tangled foliage, stifling a scream as something cool and dry slithered beneath her hand.

"Two minutes and he dies." The voice sounded close, closer than when she'd been with Melody. Tori used it as a compass, scurrying around the periphery of the village, hoping the speaker wasn't watching her every move.

"One minute."

This time the voice had faded, not much, but enough for Tori to know she'd put distance between herself and her enemy. She edged toward the clearing, her pulse thundering in her ears. The last thing she wanted to do was leave the cover of the trees, but she had no choice.

With a deep, shaky breath, she slid out of the brush and crept toward the nearest hut.

Noah saw Tori moving and gritted his teeth to keep from shouting for her to retreat. Blood seeped from a wound in his thigh, dripping onto the ground near his feet. He ignored it. Right now his focus was on Tori and on the two men she was unwittingly heading toward.

A few more minutes and he'd have had them, despite the flesh wound on his leg, despite the fact that they were well hidden behind bamboo fencing. A clear shot was all he needed, and he'd figured he had time to get it. Until Tori had crawled into the picture. Literally.

He grimaced, ignoring the low moan that sounded from the man lying trussed in the corner of the hut. Now Noah's problem wasn't how to dispose of Lao's men—it was how to get Tori out of the line of fire.

He watched her progress, praying she'd find cover and stay put. Instead she moved forward, her pace slow, steady and purposeful. Obviously, she'd believed the shouted warnings. Which proved she had little faith in Noah's ability to get them out of the mess they were in. Too bad. It would have saved them both a lot of trouble.

He moved toward the door, crouching low as he made his way down the steps. He didn't expect Lao's men to miss his exit from the hut and was prepared for the volley of shots that ripped through the morning, was counting on it as a warning to Tori.

He threw himself down the steps, landing behind the bamboo fencing, looking for the opening he needed, the chance to take out both men without risking Tori.

He rolled to the fence, his gaze searching for and finding Tori. She'd sprawled on the ground, her hands over her head, her face pressed to the ground.

She seemed to sense his gaze, turning her head to look his way. He willed her to move, to slide back into the jungle before Lao's men came up with a plan to avoid Noah's bullets and get to her. She blinked, started backing away and stopped short when a bullet slammed into the ground a few feet from her head.

Trapped. And she knew it. Noah could see it in the way her gaze jumped from place to place.

"Put down your gun, or the woman dies."

Noah might have laughed at the useless threat if the situation hadn't been so dire. Instead he held his silence, slithering along the fence, ignoring the burning pain in his leg. They were at a stalemate, but Lao's men had the advantage. Soon reinforcements would arrive and the game would be theirs. Noah had to get Tori and Melody out before then.

Another gunshot shattered the morning, and Noah glanced through the fencing again, saw that Tori had rolled his way. Good. Despite her fear she was still thinking, had come to the same conclusions as Noah, and was making her escape.

So why wasn't she heading back into the jungle?

"Wrong way, Red. Head back into the trees." He shouted the words.

"And leave you? No way." She made it to the fence, threw herself over it and landed with a muffled grunt.

"I said, go back into the forest. Melody needs you."

"She needs us both. I can't beat these guys on my own." She crawled toward him, her hair falling over her eyes, her face pale as she reached out and touched his cheek, her fingers hot against his skin. "I'm so glad you're okay."

The words were fervent, her eyes filled with worry, and he grabbed her hand, pressing a kiss to her palm. "I'm glad you're okay, too. Now go back out there and wait for the helicopter. It'll be here soon."

"Not soon enough. Besides, those men don't dare shoot me. As long as we're together you're safe."

"You're thinking backward. As long as we're together you're *not* safe. Those men have one purpose right now. Get rid of me. After they do that, they figure finding you and bringing you to Lao will be a piece of cake."

She shook her head, brushed hair from her eyes and shot him a look filled with both fear and irritation. "I'm not leaving you here."

"You're too stubborn for your own good. Get up. Get back over the fence and get out!" The tone he used had brought grown men in line with his plans.

Not Tori. She just peered over the fence and glanced back at Noah. "Come on. I'll cover you."

"You're five inches shorter and a hundred pounds lighter."

"They won't shoot at you and risk hitting me."

He wouldn't argue. "Just stay low and stay quiet."

For once she did as he asked, sinking down beside him as he pulled his gun, sighted over the fence and fired off a shot as a shadow moved behind the bamboo stakes. A short yelp of pain answered. Not a fatal shot, but enough to distract for a few seconds.

"Come on." He grabbed Tori's hand and crawled with her to the back of the fenced area. "On the count of three we go over together. Then we run."

Her eyes glowed deep brown in the dim light, filled with a quiet acceptance that seemed as much part of her nature as the determination that drove her.

Noah squeezed her hand, counted to three and dragged her over the fence with him. They ran toward the forest, zigzagging between huts, bullets slamming into the ground behind them. It was too far to safety. One of them would be hit. Noah slowed his pace, moving behind Tori, silently urging her to run faster.

A hundred feet to safety. Fifty.

A bullet whizzed past his ear, slamming into a tree with enough force to splinter the wood. Noah swung sideways, aiming at the man coming up fast behind them. He didn't have a chance to fire. Before he could pull the trigger, a shot rang out and the man collapsed.

Hawke. Noah knew it without seeing the other man—didn't even bother to look, just raced into the forest behind Tori, following her around the perimeter of the village. Hearing the sound of another shot.

"Melody!" Her voice rang through the morning.

"Here." Leaves and dirt moved, and the girl popped up a few feet from where they stood.

Tori rushed forward, pulling Melody into her arms, their profiles so similar there could be no mistaking the connection between them.

"No time for a family reunion. There are still men crawling all over this mountain. Best to take cover until the helicopter arrives." Hawke spoke, his face hard as he moved back toward the village.

"Good timing." Noah pulled white gauze from his pack, wrapped his leg as he spoke.

"I heard the fireworks and figured I might as well lend a hand."

"Simon?"

"Still playing ghost tag, but he should be here soon enough."

"How many of Lao's men did you take out?"

"Not enough." The words were harsh, Hawke's expression cold.

"DEA and the Royal Thai Police will swarm this area soon. They'll pick up whoever is left."

"Then I'd better pick up my own garbage before they get here." Hawke turned, his face devoid of emotion, the scar that bisected his cheek a white cord along his skin.

"Leave him to the police, Hawke."

The words were a harsh command and Tori tensed, her arm tightening around Melody's shoulders.

"Why? So he can live a few more years? Even a few more hours is too long for my liking."

"So you'll ruin your own life for Lao's?"

"My life was ruined long ago."

For a moment the men were silent, staring each other down. Then Noah shook his head, the movement sharp. "Leave him to the law. You don't need his blood on your hands."

"My hands are bathed in rivers of the stuff. A few more drops won't hurt." But there was something in his eyes, in his voice, that made a lie of the words.

"Won't they? Maybe it's time to let the past go. Maybe it's time to forgive and be forgiven."

"Don't waste your breath on me, Stone. Forgiveness is something I've never been granted, and something I have no intention of giving. Listen. The chopper's coming. I'll leave you to it."

He slid back into the jungle as the steady beat of chopper blades sounded from the distance.

"He's an interesting man." Tori spoke the thought aloud, surprised by the sadness she felt as she watched Hawke disappear.

"He is." Noah's voice was tight, his muscles tense as if he wanted to go after Hawke and drag him back.

"Not quite as callous as I thought."

"Hawke is the least callous man you'll ever meet. That's why he is the way he is."

"What do you mean?"

"Sorry. It's his story to tell and he doesn't tell it to anyone."

"He told it to you."

"Fever-induced rantings. Even I don't have the whole story. Come on. Let's get you two home."

A crowd of people waited at the fenced perimeter of the safe house. Obviously, Melody's rescue had been reported. Squeezed into the back of the helicopter with the teen, Tori strained forward, hoping to catch a glimpse of the Raymonds. They must be excited, relieved, so happy to know their daughter was coming home.

Pops would feel the same.

If Tori ever made it back to Lakeview. But she wouldn't think about Jack and the interrogation he was bound to put her through. Not now when there was so much to celebrate.

As soon as the chopper touched down, Melody scrambled over the seat, barely waiting until Noah climbed out before she launched herself out the door. Tori followed more slowly, the pain in her side not allowing for much more than that.

Joi and Mark were already there, holding Melody,

tugging her away from the helicopter, but never releasing their grips. Their faces glowed with excitement, all the worry and strain suddenly gone. There would still be challenges ahead, decisions about whether they could safely return to the clinic, but they'd make those decisions together.

A family.

Tori swallowed back tears of joy, refusing to acknowledge the small twinge of jealousy she felt. This was what she'd wanted—Melody with parents who loved her, who wanted the best for her and who would be there for her even in the most desperate times.

The helicopter lifted off, the churning air and thundering rotors masking the sounds of joy and triumph Tori was sure filled the air. As the roar quieted, people swarmed into the yard, calling, yelling and slapping each other on the back. Tori knew she should feel the same excitement, but all she felt was tired.

When Noah's arm slipped around her waist and he urged her toward the house, she went willingly, glad to move away from the noise.

"Tori! You're safe!" Joi greeted her, her arm still around her daughter, though she reached her other hand to clasp Tori's.

"We're all safe and once the DEA clears things up you can go back to the clinic and get back to your life." She tried to sound enthusiastic, but the words were dull.

"We wanted to talk to you about that." Mark shot a glance in Joi's direction, and Tori didn't miss the silent message that passed between them.

"What?"

"We're going home."

"Do you think that's safe? Lao might be out of commission, but there might still—"

"Not the clinic." Joi spoke, her voice just a little shaky. "We're going back to Virginia."

"For a visit?"

"For as long as God keeps us there."

"But the clinic is everything you've always wanted. You planned it for years. Worked there from its conception." They couldn't really be leaving, not the clinic they'd founded, the one they'd helped build, the one they'd planned for years.

"True. But it's only a part of our lives. We've already spoken to Dr. Graw. He's agreed to take over as director while we continue to do fund-raising from the States." Mark sounded almost relieved, as if a weight had been lifted from his shoulders.

"I can't believe this. You love the clinic."

"No. We love its mission, we love the service it provides, but we love our families, too, and my mom hasn't been in the best of health lately. Mark and I have been feeling God urging us to move on for a while now. We'd actually already discussed the details with Dr. Graw. This has just pushed us to act a little sooner."

What to say? How to respond? Despite what they said, Tori knew the truth. She'd come for a visit and the result had been chaos for the Raymonds. Now they were leaving a home they loved because of the danger she'd brought into their lives. "I'm sorry."

"For what?" Joi looked genuinely surprised.

"I—"

"I think what Tori meant to say, is that she's happy for you. I'm happy for you, too." Noah spoke from behind Tori, and she nodded, hoping the Raymonds would take her assent as enthusiasm for their plan.

Chatter, laughter, joy. Tori could barely keep up with the emotions that filled the safe house as Melody was examined by her mother and declared unhurt. An hour passed, calls were made and Tori felt only vaguely a part of it, her body numb, her mind foggy. She barely noticed when Noah spoke into his radio or when the sound of a helicopter roared through the house.

It was only when the door to the living room flew open and a man tumbled in, falling in a bloody heap on the floor, that Tori realized what all the commotion was about.

His face had been beaten almost beyond recognition, but the paunchy body and slicked-back hair gave away his identity. Tori stumbled up from the chair she was sitting in, dizzy, not trusting Lao to stay down.

Hawke stepped into the room behind him, his face a cold mask. "Take him now or there won't be anything left to prosecute."

There was no doubting the truth of the words, and Noah grabbed Lao's arm. "Up. Now. Or you're a dead man."

That seemed to galvanize Lao, and he scrambled up, backing away from Hawke with an expression so filled with terror, Noah knew he must recognize the man whose family he had destroyed over a decade ago.

Hawke shot him one last, venomous look and stalked back outside.

"I demand a doctor. I demand the police."

"The first will have to wait, but I think I can arrange the second for you." Noah kept his hand firm on Lao's arm and turned to Tori.

"It shouldn't take me long, but stay here, one way or another."

"Where would I go?"

"Home?"

"If I thought I could get past airport security, that's exactly what I'd do."

"Then I guess it's good you don't think you can." He grinned and steered Lao out the door.

Chapter Nineteen

"Lao's drug-running days are over." Mark's comment drew Tori's attention to the Raymonds who'd watched the exchange in silence.

"Then I guess something good came out of all this." Did she sound as weary as she felt?

"A lot of good. Lao's organization is one of the Wa's biggest distributors in Thailand. Closing down his operations won't stop the trafficking of heroin, but it'll put a dent in it." Mark raked a hand through his hair, rubbed a finger along the bridge of his nose. "I think the DEA owes you big-time, Tori. From what I've heard they've been trying to get the proof they needed to close Lao down for years."

"Owe me? They think I worked for him."

"Not after this they don't." Joi released the hold she had on her daughter and walked over to Tori. "You did good, Tori. I'm so proud of you."

"Not me. Noah, Hawke and Simon. I just watched things unfold."

"Somehow I don't believe that, though I have to admit Noah seems like a good guy."

"He is. I don't know how we would have found Melody without him."

"That's why God brought him here."

A week ago, Tori would have ignored the comment. Now she couldn't deny the truth of it—that God had brought Noah here. And that He'd worked and moved and shaped each moment, kept them safe, given them reason to hope.

And brought them all together once again.

"Okay. Lao's in custody. It's time to head out." Noah stepped back into the room, and Tori's heart tripped at the sight of him. Would she see him again when this was over? Did she want to? She turned away too quickly, her head pounding with the movement.

"Where to?" Mark's question seemed to come from a distance, and Tori tried to shake away the darkness that danced at the edges of her vision.

"We've got a police escort back to the airport. We'll fly to Bangkok from there. Jack's already on his way to the embassy."

"We'll go back to the clinic first. Pack our things." Joi worried at her lower lip, her eyes moist with what could only be tears. Despite what she'd said, leaving would be hard.

"I wish I could let you do that, but it isn't safe. We've still got to round up the rest of Lao's organization. Even if we had them all in custody, we can't rule out the Wa sending men across the border. Losing Lao is going to cost them big. They may decide to retaliate. The DEA is sending people out to gather your belongings. They'll do a good job for you."

"But—"

"He's right, honey." Mark cut into whatever protest

Joi planned to make. "Possessions aren't nearly as important as your safety and Melody's."

She nodded. "Or yours. So let's go pack the few things we brought with us. Ready, Mel?"

The teenager nodded and the three walked from the room.

"They'll be fine." Noah's words drew Tori from her thoughts, and she turned to face him once again.

"Will they?"

"Of course. They have each other. They have their faith."

"I still wish—"

"If wishes were horses, beggars would ride, Red."

"My grandfather used to tell me that a hundred times a day."

"Yeah? I think I'm going to like your grandfather."

"Who says you're going to meet him?"

"You still owe me a steak and seafood dinner, remember?"

"You haven't gotten me home yet."

"But I will. And when I do, I'll be coming to your house to pick you up before we have dinner and I'll meet Pops. Think he'll mind if I call him that?"

"Yes." But she smiled thinking about it.

"Car here." A young Thai man peeked into the room, his tan face flushed pink with excitement.

"Thanks. Stay here for another minute, Red. I'm going to speak with the police one more time before we leave. Make sure they're transporting Lao to Bangkok." He walked from the room and Tori leaned against the wall, too tired to move.

"Hey, kid, you look beat." Mark strode toward her, his eyes filled with concern. "You okay?"

"Nothing a few days' rest won't cure."

He ignored her response and placed his hand on her forehead. "You're burning up."

"Just overheated."

"Just sick. Forget Bangkok. We'll take you to the hospital in Chiang Mai. It's closer."

"No! It's too close. Too easy for Lao's men to find us there."

"What's going on?" Joi and Melody stepped into the room, Joi's gaze going from Tori to Mark and back again.

"Tori's sick. I want to take her to Chiang Mai for treatment."

"And I said I'm fine. We can't risk being in Chiang Mai when some of Lao's men are on the loose."

"So? You need treatment now. Not three hours from now. I'm going to tell Noah there's been a change in plans. Melody and Joi will go to Bangkok. You and I are going to Chiang Mai."

Tori grabbed his shirtsleeve, stopping him before he could walk away. "No. You need to be with your family. Not with me."

Mark's brow furrowed, the lines around his eyes deepening. "You are my family."

"You know what I mean."

"No. I don't think I do."

"Melody's your daughter. Joi's your wife. I'm just…" She floundered, seeing the hurt in Joi's face, the surprise in Melody's and the anger in Mark's. "What I mean is—"

"Wait." Mark held up a hand, confusion and frustration clear on his face. "Tori, if we've ever given you the impression that all you were to us was the woman who gave birth to our daughter—"

"No, of course you didn't."

"Let me finish. I know Joi's said it before, but maybe you need to hear it from me, too. If you'd never given Melody to us, we'd still be family. There's a connection. Something meant to be. Joi felt it first, but I knew it soon after. Before we realized you were pregnant, before we ever discussed adopting Melody, I felt that you were meant to be part of our lives, that God intended for us to be a family."

The sincerity in the words was unmistakable, the love in his eyes something that Tori had seen a thousand times and never recognized.

Her throat clogged with too many emotions and she leaned forward to hug him. "You've never made me feel like an outsider. I did that all by myself."

She stepped back, trying to smile. "It's going to be good to have you living closer."

"Which still doesn't solve the problem of where you're going to be treated." Joi pressed her hand against Tori's forehead. "You really are warm."

"I'll be okay."

"Everyone ready? We've got two cars. Tori's riding with me."

Noah's announcement ended the argument. Perhaps because the Raymonds were too tired and overwhelmed to continue it. So was Tori.

She climbed into the backseat of a black sedan, nodding at the driver, her hands fumbling as she tried to get the end of the seat belt to click into place.

"Let me." Noah slid in next to Tori, reaching over and taking the seat belt from her lax fingers and buckling it for her.

"I hope the Raymonds will be okay." The words slipped out, and a tear slid down Tori's cheek.

"Why do you think they won't."

"They're leaving everything they love, everything they worked so hard for."

"And they're following God's will for their lives."

"God's will? What about Lao's will? The Wa's will? Mark and Joi aren't leaving because of God. They're leaving because they're afraid."

"They didn't let fear stop them when they came here five years ago. Why assume they're doing it now?"

"Because I can't see that it's anything else."

"Because you don't *want* to see it as anything else. If fear's sending them running, you can understand, sympathize, maybe find a reason to blame yourself or God. If He's leading them away and they're going, despite their love for the clinic and the people they treat, they're showing you a way to live that you can't and won't accept."

"You don't know what you're talking about." Tori turned away, staring out the window, tears still falling despite her best effort to force them back.

Noah didn't speak, the silence between them stretching taut, filled with things he wanted to say but didn't dare. He touched her cheek, let his hand slide around so it cupped her jaw, urging her to look at him again. "Maybe things aren't working out the way you'd like, but that doesn't mean things aren't the way they should be. The Raymonds have been thinking about this move for a while. They have peace that they're doing what they should."

"Will they in a year? In two? Ten? If the clinic closes down, will they still think they did the right thing?"

"They'll know they did what they were meant to do. That'll be enough."

"I wish I believed that."

"Don't wish, Red. Believe."

"That's not such an easy thing."

"It's as easy as you let it be."

She shook her head, a smile curving her lips even as the tears fell faster. "You don't think anything is impossible, do you?"

"No. Especially not when someone like you sets her mind to the task."

"I think you have more confidence in me than I have in myself."

"I have enough confidence for both of us. Come here." He pressed her head to his shoulder, stroking the tangled hair that fell down her back. "Give it a week or two. You'll see how it all falls into place, and when you do, God's stamp will be all over it."

"I think it already is." The words were mumbled against his chest, barely audible above the hum of the car's engine. They surprised him, and Noah looked down into Tori's face. Her eyes were closed, her breathing deep and even. Already asleep. And just when things were getting interesting.

Noah smiled and leaned his head back against the seat.

The quiet hum of voices and soft swish of fabric drifted into Tori's dreams, urging her to wake. She'd rather not. For the first time in days she felt warm, no shivers racking her body, no pain slicing along her nerves, something soft beneath her head. Not the car, then, with Noah riding beside her.

"Tori?" A voice she recognized, but not Noah's. "You hear me, gal?"

"Pops." Her throat scratched with the effort, her mouth too dry.

"That's right. Dragged my sorry behind all the way from Lakeview and you're too lazy to get up and say hello." The same teasing tone she'd heard for years, edged with a note of worry that had Tori forcing her eyes open.

She blinked against bright light, trying to focus on Pops.

"Now, that's more like it. Told those doctors you'd wake up when I got here." He smiled, but there were tears in his eyes, his lined face close enough to touch if Tori had the energy to lift her hand. She didn't.

"Where am I?"

"Hospital in Bangkok. Had everybody scared. Thought that infection just might do you in, but I told them you were too stubborn to quit." His voice broke and he stood up, clearing his throat and pacing to a wide window.

"How long?"

"Three days."

"Melody?"

"Right as rain. Saw her last night. Raymonds met me at the airport. Brought me here."

"So they're safe?" Tori shifted, trying to sit up, but someone pressed her back against the pillow.

"Lie still."

Noah. Tori turned her head, saw him in a chair beside the bed, and her pulse raced with recognition and pleasure. "You're here."

"Where else would I be?"

"Home. Going back to your life."

"Not before I make sure you're ready to go back to yours. Now, stay put while I get the nurse."

"Why is it you're always telling me to stay put?"

"Because I always know if I don't, you'll be running around getting into trouble." He smiled, brushed a kiss against her cheek and stepped out of the room.

He'd barely disappeared through the door when Pops spoke. "Seems like a nice guy."

"He is." Tori's eyelids were leaden and she forced them to stay open.

"Cares about you a lot."

"He's doing his job."

"Don't think so. Guy named Jack came in last night, saw Noah and asked what he was still doing in Bangkok. Job was over, he said. Noah could get back to his life."

"Noah's an honorable man."

"Sure is. So I'm thinking you'd better hang on to him."

"Pops, I—" But any protest she might have made was cut off by the arrival of the doctor and nurse.

Noah was right behind them, his gaze on Tori as he settled back down into the chair. "Glad you're back, Red."

"Me, too. Surprised you're here."

"I said I'd make sure you got home."

"How long will that be?" The questions stung her throat and made her long to close her eyes and drift back to sleep.

"A few more days, Ms. Riley. It takes time and rest to heal the body." The doctor pressed his stethoscope to her chest, listening intently.

"How's she sounding, Doc?" Pops edged closer, staring down at Tori, worry still lining his face.

"Better. Much better. You're strong. We'll have you

home in no time at all." He picked up one hand, examined her wrist. "Good. Good. Yes, much better."

"When are you going home, Noah?" The question slipped out, and she wondered if she should have asked, if she was showing too much interest, maybe even possessiveness.

He didn't seem to care. Just smiled and exchanged a look with Pops. A look Tori wasn't sure she liked. "A day or two. I've got some business to attend to in the States. My brother thinks he's found some property for the dog-training center we're opening. Wants me to come look before someone else scoops it up."

"Good news."

"It is, but not as good as knowing you're doing better." He linked his fingers with Tori's, watching as the doctor examined her other wrist, shone a light in her eyes. "What do you think, Dr. Janakhundee?"

"I think all those prayers have worked. Your friend is going to be just fine. Home in a week. Then plenty of rest. Good food. You'll make sure she gets that?" He eyed both men. And both nodded.

The doctor smiled and closed the chart he'd been writing. "You're a lucky lady having these two men care so much for you."

"I know."

Pops hurried forward, walking the doctor to the door and stepping out into the hall with him, the nurse close on their heels.

Noah remained sitting, his hand still around Tori's. "Sam's a good guy."

"Funny, he was just saying the same about you."

"I told you we'd get along."

"You did." Her eyes drifted closed, and Noah's fingers brushed her cheek. "Rest for a while. I'll be here when you wake up."

And he would. Tori knew it. Just as she knew Pops would be there.

Images swirled behind her eyes, all the things that had happened over the past ten days, the worry, the fear, the relief when they'd found Melody alive and well. Those moments before she'd left Melody and gone into the village after Noah. That strong, sure feeling that Melody would be okay. That God was there and would lead her safely home. "You were right, you know."

"About?"

She opened her eyes, met Noah's worried gaze. "When you said God's stamp was on everything. It is. I don't know why it took me so long to see it."

"Not so long. Just a few days."

"Years. Not days. I thought God had turned His back on me. Now I think maybe it was the other way around. Maybe I've been turning my back on Him. Maybe He's been working His will in my life all along and I just couldn't see it because I was facing the wrong direction." Her words faded at the end, the effort to keep talking too much.

Noah brushed hair from her forehead, his fingers lingering in her hair. "So maybe it's time to face the direction you really want to go. Now stop talking and rest. I'm never going to be able to collect my steak and seafood dinner if you don't get well and get back to Lakeview."

"You've already met Pops. No need to come."

"Trying to weasel out of dinner, Red?"

She smiled, imagining Noah arriving in Lakeview

and the stir that would cause. "Looking forward to it. Maybe if I'm seen with you, the Lakeview ladies will stop asking me who I'm dating and when I'm getting married."

Laughter filled the air—warm, rich, and inviting. "I knew I'd prove useful to you eventually. Now rest. You need to heal."

She wanted to keep her eyes open, wanted to listen for a few more minutes to Noah's laughter, imagine for a while that he really did plan to come to Lakeview. But the effort to stay awake was too much and her eyes drifted closed.

Chapter Twenty

Three weeks later

"And you never saw him again?"

"Just once. I woke up that night and he was there. Reading his Bible. We only spoke for a minute. That was it. I haven't seen him since. Not that I expected to." Tori prayed forgiveness for the half-truth and handed Perky to his owner. "Looks like Perky's going to be okay."

Edna Murphy nodded vigorously, her topknot bun sliding precariously forward. "I'm so glad he's going to be okay. But I'm worried about you. There you were, lost in the jungle—"

"Not lost, Ms. Edna. Noah knew exactly where we were."

"Lost in the jungle with a man who knew where he was and what had to be done. I've heard he had black hair and eyes to die for."

"The story's being embellished as it gets passed along." But not by much.

"Still, it sounds so…romantic." A tinge of pink added color to the former teacher's cheeks.

"It might sound romantic, but it was more scary than anything else."

"You're braver than I am. Going after Melody. Making sure she was okay." Edna stroked her Yorkshire terrier's head, her faded blue eyes wide with admiration.

"Not so brave. I just did what I had to do." They were words she'd been saying almost nonstop as she treated patient after patient, most with vague symptoms and no sign of illness. Returning to work had seemed like a good idea during her long days of recovery. Now, with the waiting room overflowing for the second day in a row, Tori wasn't so sure she'd made the right decision.

"Well, I, for one, am proud of you."

"Thank you, Ms. Edna. Now I really must—"

"Sam's proud of you, too. To hear him tell the story, you saved Melody single-handedly."

"I had lots of help."

"Yes, that good-looking CIA agent."

"DEA."

"Right. Still, it had to be difficult, what with your injuries."

Tori bit back a sigh of impatience and glanced at the clock. "Thanks for being so conscientious about Perky's care, Ms. Edna. Not many owners would bring a dog in just because he'd ingested crumbs from a devil's food cake."

"Well, I do try to take care of him. He's such a sweet little dog."

"That he is. I'll see you at church Sunday." She pulled the examining room door open.

"Speaking of church. Our Sunday school class is doing a study on the book of Job. Persevering during trying circumstances. You know the stuff."

"Of course."

"Well, now that you're attending Grace Christian again, we thought you might be willing to speak to the group."

"I'd be happy to. Why don't we pick a time on Sun—"

"Oh, now is good. Just let me get my calendar."

Tori glanced at the clock again, a dull thud of pain building in the back of her head. She was behind. Really behind. "Ms. Edna, I really don't—"

"Dr. Riley, we've got a very impatient Persian cat in room three." Martha Gabler appeared, her trim, athletic figure and sandy blond hair vibrating with energy.

"Thanks, Marti. I'll take care of that now."

"Oh, my. I guess I've overstayed Perky's visit. We'll talk more Sunday." Edna hurried away, ready, no doubt, to share what little she'd learned.

"Anything I can get for you, Doc?"

"A little of whatever you're taking."

"Taking?"

"All that energy. It must be coming from somewhere."

"Yeah, a million weekends spent sitting in front of the TV wondering when Prince Charming will ride in to rescue me from complete and utter boredom." Martha grinned, dimples flashing in both cheeks.

"Complete and utter boredom has its perks."

"Perks that do not include handsome strangers running to rescue me from bad guys. Come on, you're looking green around the gills. Get some juice from your office, take a load off your feet. I'll keep Horatio and Pamela occupied."

"Pam Snyder and Horatio the king?"

"That would be them."

Tori pictured the svelte blonde and her spoiled cat and groaned. "I'll be there in five."

"I've got a better idea. Why don't we cancel the rest of today's appointments? Send everyone home. It's not like any of the pets out there are actually sick."

"I'll see them anyway. Go on and stall Pam." Tori stepped inside her office and closed the door before Martha could argue further.

Fatigue tugged at her body, begging her to sit down in a chair, put her feet up and close her eyes, but sleep wasn't what she needed. She needed to keep busy. Otherwise she spent too much time thinking about Thailand, about Lao and the men who'd tortured her. About Noah.

She grimaced and grabbed a bottle of apple juice from the cooler near her desk. The sweet, cool liquid washed down her throat, but did little to lift her spirits. Neither did the flower arrangements that covered every available surface in the room. Pinks, blues, bright reds—there were so many colors, Tori felt dizzy looking at them. Maybe the church could use them as pulpit flowers. Ben Avery, her pastor, had been so kind since her return, so happy to answer her questions, to pray with her and for her. It would make Tori happy to fill his office and the pulpit with flowers. It would make her more happy to finish the day.

And to see Noah again.

She pushed the last thought aside, refusing to let herself imagine seeing him again. He'd gone on with his life. It was time for her to do the same.

"Ready?" Martha peeked in the room, her sharp gaze taking in Tori's appearance. "You're still pale."

"I'm fine. Let's get this over with." Tori pasted a smile on her face and stepped out of her office.

Two hours later, Tori was still tired and ready to go home, but able to finally see an end to the day. All but one exam room was empty, patients treated and released, owners fed just enough information to keep them happy. The hum and bustle that had permeated the clinic earlier had been replaced by the roar of a vacuum and the soft laughter of the staff getting ready to leave for the night.

"Who's in five?" Tori grabbed the chart off the door and glanced at the paperwork.

"Six puppies. Owner just moved to the area. The pups have had their shots and got a clean bill of health a few weeks ago."

"And I'm seeing them because…?"

"Probably the same reason you've seen every other patient we've had in today." Martha handed Tori a cup of coffee. "Drink. You look like you're going to fall over."

"Not quite that bad, I hope." Tori brushed stray curls behind her ears, straightened the lapels of the white lab coat she wore and pushed open the door to the room. A brown-and-black ball of fur scurried by, heading for the open door and adventure.

"Sorry, buddy. No escapes today." She scooped the puppy up, turned to face the owner and froze.

"Good catch, Red."

He looked the same—tall, lean, black hair a little too long and eyes a deep blue-green.

"Noah."

"I was hoping you'd remember."

"How could I forget?"

Noah grinned, taking the puppy from her arms and putting it down on the floor. "Go play, Hercules."

"Hercules?"

"Runt of the litter. I wanted to give him a big name."

"What about the others? Have you named them?" She focused her attention on the puppies, afraid if she looked too long, Noah would see the longing and the relief in her eyes.

"Of course. Jazz, Trouble, Dare, Maverick and Mouse. Mouse is the biggest, but she's timid. Time'll tell if she's up for the challenge of search and rescue."

"So you did it? You've got the land and you're opening the training center?" Tori grabbed his arm, excitement making her forget that they were nothing to one another.

"We did. Ten miles outside of Lakeview. We're breaking ground next week and are looking to open in a year."

"Lakeview? You've moved to the area."

"Yeah. The old Sheffield place."

"I know it."

"Then you know it's a beautiful piece of property."

"It is." The thought of Noah living so close filled her with more excitement than she wanted to admit. She looked at the tumbling, wrestling puppies again, trying to calm her racing thoughts. "So, Martha says you need me to take a look at the puppies."

"I think you know why I'm really here." He took a step closer, his hand cupping her cheek, his eyes scanning her face. "Your bruises are almost gone."

"I heal quickly."

"That's not what Sam's been telling me. He's been worried."

"You've been talking to Sam?"

"I wanted to give you time to think things through. Sam's been keeping me informed. I think he enjoys playing spy."

"I should be angry." She put her hand on his wrist, intending to push his arm away, but her fingers betrayed her, curving around his warm skin.

"Are you?"

"Maybe. Who I talk to, how much time I need, that's my choice, not yours or Pops."

He nodded, dropping his hand away from her face, but linking his fingers with hers, the connection between them as strong and sure as it had been during their time in Thailand.

"It was real, wasn't it?" The words slipped out and Tori bit her lip to keep from saying more.

"Yeah, it was."

"I thought maybe everything that happened, all the fear and worry…"

"Had you building things up in your mind?"

"Something like that." She released his hand, crouched down to scratch one of the puppies behind the ear.

"It's nothing so simple as that, Red." He crouched beside her. "I knew when I took the assignment that God had something important for me to do in Thailand."

"Saving Melody and closing down Lao's operation was that."

"True. But what's between us is important, too. And I'm not going to let it fade away."

Tori's hand trembled as she picked up the puppy and pulled it against her chest, burying her nose in warm, brown fur. "I don't have a very good track record with men."

"So Sam's been telling me. Two broken engagements in three years."

"Pops and I are going to have a serious talk when I get home."

Noah grinned. "Don't blame Sam. I'm pretty good at getting information when I set my mind to it."

"Then I guess we're going to have a serious talk, too."

"I thought you'd never ask." He rose, pulling her along with him. "Let's go."

"Go where?"

"Dinner. Seafood and steak. I do better at talking when I've got something in my stomach. Besides, we had a deal, remember?"

"What about the puppies?"

"Sam's **babysitting**."

"He knows you're here?"

"Not yet, but I figure we'll stop by and say hello. I have a feeling he'll jump at the chance to watch the puppies if it means the two of us go out to dinner together."

"Noah, I…" Tori's heart raced with fear and with anticipation. She didn't know which she felt more of.

He picked up two of the squirming bundles of fur and put them in a large carrier before turning to face her, tension radiating from him, his jaw tight. "You're scared. I am, too. But there's no rush. No hurry. We have all the time in the world to get to know each other, to decide if this really is God's plan or if it's just ours. Let's take this first step and trust that He's brought us together for a reason. Whatever that might be."

He must have practiced those words, prepared for her argument. Tori wasn't sure if she should be touched or irritated that he knew her so well. She only knew that she was tempted to do exactly what he suggested.

Say no! The old Tori shouted the words silently. *You're going to get hurt again and you'll only have yourself to blame.*

But she wasn't the old Tori any longer. Thailand had changed her. Faith had changed her. She took a deep, steadying breath and put the puppy she held into the carrier. "There's a good restaurant in Roanoke."

The tension in Noah eased and he smiled. "Seafood?"

"And steak."

"Then I guess we'd better get moving." He put the last puppy in the carrier and lifted it. "Just one more thing."

"What's that?"

"Thanks." He brushed a kiss against her lips, the gesture sweet, warm and filled with promise.

"Dr. Ri... Oh, my." Martha Gabler stood in the doorway, her eyes wide, her cheeks pink. "Oh. My."

"Marti, this is Noah Stone."

"*The* Noah Stone?"

"That would be the one. Noah, this is Martha Gabler. A good friend and priceless receptionist."

"Nice to meet you, Ms. Gabler."

"Call me Marti. Everyone else does."

"And you can call me Noah."

"Noah, then. I'd love to stay and chat, but I'm thinking I'd better get home and put my feet up."

"Put your feet up?" Tori took a hard look at her receptionist, afraid the other woman might be ill.

"Yeah, if we thought today was bad, wait until Lakeview gets wind of the newest development in the Tori Riley saga. We'll be swamped tomorrow. Psychotic cats, depressed guinea pigs."

"I doubt they'll hear the news for a while." Tori stripped off her lab coat and went to hang it on the back of the exam room door.

"Tori, honey, do you really think I'm going to keep this choice piece of news to myself?" Martha hurried to the front door of the clinic. "Just think of what this will do to Pamela. Knowing that just moments after she departed the clinic, Noah Stone arrived."

She paused for breath, her excitement waning only slightly. "Of course, if you tell me to keep things to myself, I will. It'll be torture, but I'll do it."

Tori looked at Noah, saw the smile in his eyes, the humor dancing at the corners of his mouth. "Go ahead and tell the world, Marti."

Then she linked her arm with Noah's and took the first step toward wherever God would lead.

* * * * *

Dear Reader,

Life is filled with choices—stay or move, spend or save, take a new job or remain at an old one. If you're like me, you're faced with decisions every day. Sometimes it's easy to choose what path to take. Other times all the paths look the same, no choice better or worse than any other. That's when fear can take hold. We worry that we'll make the wrong choice, that somehow our decision will lead us to a place we shouldn't be. Fortunately, God is in control. He can and will lead us toward the goal—a life lived well for Him.

That's what happens to Tori Riley. When a trip to Thailand puts her in the path of one of the region's most notorious drug cartels, she wonders if what she thought was the right decision is actually the worst mistake she's ever made. As she races through the jungle of Mae Hong Son, she must trust DEA Agent Noah Stone to keep her safe. His steadfast faith forces Tori to reassess her own wavering beliefs. Only then can she see God's hand guiding her decisions and leading forward into His perfect plan for her life.

I'm sure you can sense how enthusiastic I am about this story! I hope you'll share my excitement as you join Tori and Noah on their journey. And when the journey is complete, I'd love to hear from you. Drop me a line at shirlee@shirleemccoy.com.

Blessings,

Shirlee McCoy

Look for the next book in the LAKEVIEW *series,*
WHEN SILENCE FALLS, in March,
from Shirlee McCoy and Love Inspired Suspense!
Turn the page for a sneak peek...

Chapter One

Piper Sinclair knew a bad thing when she saw it, and right now she was seeing it. A dozen women, all in various colors and styles of spandex, sat on bamboo mats staring with undisguised adoration at a slim woman whose banal smile set Piper's teeth on edge. A whiteboard at the front of the room stated the purpose of the meeting—"Love Yourself to Weight Loss." To either side of the whiteboard, long candle-laden tables sent up a steady stream of vanilla scented air.

"Forget it. I've changed my mind." Piper did a U-turn and tried to exit the room, but Gabriella Webber blocked her retreat, her sweet, wouldn't-hurt-a-fly face set in mutinous lines.

"You can't change your mind. You promised."

"I wouldn't have if you'd told me what this seminar was about."

"I did tell you what it was about."

"You said a weight-loss meeting. You didn't say new age mumbo-jumbo." The words were a quiet hiss, but from the look on Gabby's face, Piper might as well have shouted.

"Shhhhh! Dr. Lillian will hear you."

"I'm barely whispering."

But the slim, smiling woman was hurrying across the room as if she had heard the exchange. "Welcome, ladies. I'm Dr. Sidney Lillian. Please, have a seat. We'll be ready to begin in just a few minutes."

Piper wanted to tell the doctor she wouldn't be staying, but Gabby was staring at her with such hopeful pleading she didn't have the heart to walk out.

"Thank you, Dr. Lillian. Come on, Gabby. Let's find a seat." Piper chose a mat close to the back of the room and sat down.

Gabby lowered herself onto a mat a few feet away. Then leaned over and grabbed Piper's arm, her dark eyes brimming with excitement. "I can't believe we're really doing this. If this class works as well as it's supposed to, I'll be slim and trim by Christmas. Just in time to find a New Year's date."

"Gabby…" But what could Piper say? That losing weight wouldn't help Gabby find Mr. Right? That Mr. Right didn't exist? That all Piper had ever found were a lot of Mr. Wrongs, all gussied up to look like what they weren't? "You'll have a New Year's date whether you lose the weight or not. You always do."

"I know. I just want this year to be different."

Meaning she wanted commitment, love, marriage. All the things women of almost thirty typically wanted. All the things Piper had decided she could do without. She smiled anyway, patting Gabby's arm. "It will be."

"I hope you're right." Gabby settled back onto her mat, a smile brightening her face as the class began.

Piper's bamboo mat was uncomfortable, and the strange love-talk the class was forced to participate in was even more so. *I love my belly. I love my hips.* Since when did one need to affirm affection for each and every body part in order to lose weight? By the time the forty-minute session wound to an end, Piper was ready to ask for a refund on her money and her time.

"Are there any questions before we adjourn?" Dr. Lillian's voice was warm honey, but her eyes were cold.

Piper started to raise her hand and got an elbow to the ribs for her effort.

"Don't you dare." Gabby hissed the warning, her eyes shooting daggers.

Piper grinned, shrugged, and let her hand drop.

Another woman—a plump blonde with a pretty face and striking blue eyes—raised her hand. "Dr. Lillian?"

"Yes, Piper?"

Despite her gut-level dislike of the woman, Piper felt a twinge of sympathy for Dr. Lillian as the blonde's cheeks stained pink and a frown line appeared between her brows. "I'm not—"

She never had the chance to finish. One minute scented candles and soft music created an atmosphere of gentle serenity. The next, a dark blur raced into sight. A man. Medium height, wearing jeans, a faded T-shirt and a mask. Carrying a gun. A gun!

He grabbed the blonde who'd moments before been pink with embarrassment or anger. Now she was pale as paper, her eyes wide with fear.

Someone screamed. Others took up the chorus.

"Enough!"

The silence was immediate and pulsing with terror.

"That's better. Now everyone just stay put and you

won't get hurt." He inched toward the door, his arm locked around the blonde's neck, his pale yellow-green eyes staring out from behind the ski mask. Crocodile eyes. And like a crocodile, he had no intention of letting his prey escape alive.

The thoughts flashed through Piper's mind, demanding action. She took a step toward the man. "Let her go."

A mouse could have made more noise. She tried again. "Let her go. Before you make more trouble for yourself."

His reptilian gaze raked over Piper and dismissed her as no threat. Still, the gun he held never wavered. He kept it pointed toward the group as he took one step after another, slowly, inexorably pulling his victim to the door. Ten steps and he'd be there. Nine.

The long sleeve of his T-shirt hiked up around his forearm, revealing a snake tattoo that coiled around his wrist and up toward his elbow. The deep greens and reds of the serpent seemed to undulate, the gold eyes almost exactly matching the eyes of the gunman—hard. Evil.

The other women must have sensed the same. Each was frozen in place, eyes fixed on the gun as if staring hard enough would keep it from firing.

Eight steps. Seven. Soon he'd pull the woman out the door and into the parking lot. He'd disappear, the woman with him.

Six.

The smart thing to do would be to wait until the man walked outside and then call for help. It's what Piper's brother Jude would expect her to do. A New York City cop, he knew the best way to respond in a crisis, and he'd drilled her on everything from natural disasters to hostage situations.

Five. Four.

The blonde's eyes were wide with terror, begging someone, anyone, to stop what was happening. Piper couldn't ignore the plea. She stepped forward again, praying for wisdom and for help. "Hey, you're holding her too tight. She can't breathe. She's turning blue!"

The hysteria in her voice was real, and the blonde did her part, moaning, dropping her weight against the arm that held her. The gunman glanced down and that was all the chance Piper needed. She leaped forward, raising her leg in a roundhouse kick she'd been practicing for months. Hard. Fast. To the wrist. Just the way her brother Tristan had taught her. The gun flew from the man's hand, landing with a soft thud on the floor a few feet away. Piper dove for it, her fingers brushing against metal just as a hand hooked onto her arm and threw her sideways.

She slammed into a table, her head crashing into the wall, candles spilling onto the table and floor. Stars shot upward in hot, greedy fingers of light.

"Fire!" Gabby's scream cut through Piper's daze and she blinked, focusing on the gauzy curtains now being consumed by the flames.

All around her the room echoed with noise—women calling to one another, feet pounding on the floor, an alarm screaming to life. Dr. Lillian stood amidst the chaos, calmly speaking on a cell phone. Most likely calling for help.

"Piper! Come on, we've got to get out of here." Gabby grabbed her arm and pulled her toward the door.

"Where's the guy with the gun? The woman?"

"Already gone. He let go of her when you kicked the gun out of his hand. I still can't believe you did it. I think you might have broken his wrist."

The thought made Piper light-headed. Or maybe it was the knock on the head she'd gotten. Whatever the case, she felt dizzy and sick. "I wasn't trying to. I just wanted him to drop the gun."

"Well, he did. But he picked it up again before he ran. Now stop talking and move faster. This whole place could go up in flames any minute."

Outside, daylight had faded to blue-purple dusk, the hazy mid-July heat humid and cloying. People hugged the curb of the parking lot, staring at the smoke billowing from the three-level brownstone that housed Dr. Lillian's practice. In the distance, sirens wailed and screamed, growing closer with each breath. Soon Lynchburg's finest would arrive. If God was good, and Piper knew He was, Grayson wouldn't be with them. The last thing she needed, or wanted, was her oldest brother's raised eyebrow and overburdened sigh.

What she needed, what she wanted, was to walk away. To leave the burning building, the crying, gasping blonde and shell-shocked, spandex-clad women behind, go home, and forget any of this had ever happened. But just as Jude had taught her to be cautious and Tristan had taught her to fight, Grayson had taught her responsibility. She was here for the duration. No matter how fervently she wished otherwise.

She sighed, moved into the crowd of people, and waited for help to arrive.

Love Inspired® SUSPENSE

TITLES AVAILABLE NEXT MONTH

Don't miss these two stories in February

THE DANGER WITHIN by Valerie Hansen
Faith at the Crossroads

Meat-and-potatoes rancher Michael Vance needed help. His ranch foreman had disappeared, his housekeeper had sprained her ankle and his cattle were not looking all that healthy. With all the extra work around the place, he was forced to turn to bohemian beauty Layla Dixon for veterinary help. Will their unlikely partnership become a partnership...for life?

STORMCATCHER by Colleen Rhoads
Great Lakes Legends

Uncovering a *modern-day* crime scene was not how marine archaeologist Wynne Baxter expected to use her diving skills. Yet when handsome family friend Simon Lassiter fell under suspicion in the death of his cousin and former fiancée, Wynne vowed to help him learn the truth, even though it meant risking everything in Superior's stormy waters.

LISCNM0106